THE WORLD WITHIN

Inner Earth and the Fight for Justice

By

Angela Hutcheon

Cover and Logo: Angela Hutcheon
Printed by Angela Hutcheon

Alicante, Spain

1st Edition Angela Hutcheon 2020

PREFACE

Being a metaphysical person the inspiration for this book could be said to have come from a link to the spiritual world, receiving messages, better known as "channelling", and tapping into my own imagination. This book came about by my own interest in new age articles about Inner Earth or Hollow Earth and the imagination grew from there.

It was not easy writing this book, well, it was but making this book more readable to the reader, a story was created involving two girls; one who had escaped to the Surface of Earth and her sister, who remained in Inner Earth and what brought them together.

THANK YOU TO

Catherine W. Dunne for her help and being there to guide me and encourage me.

My husband for being there to support me and encouraging me to follow my dreams.

INTRODUCTION

The story begins with the main character Carrie who is living in a busy town, in a shared student's accommodation with her best college friend, but never revealed a hidden secret about herself.

The girls were planning their Senior Prom Celebrations and out of the blue, Carrie is contacted by her sister, who is in distress and must leave to try and help her sister. The story revolves around their cruel and dangerous and manipulative father.

Carrie's sister is kidnapped. Carrie must find a way to rescue her. Unintentionally, her close friends are being dragged in ... and the secret Carrie carried with her for years, is now being revealed. A secret, that brings everyone involved, down into the unheard-of regions of this planet Earth, deep inside into Inner Earth.

Having been kidnapped as well, her friends find a way to help escape the clutches of their father Carl, and soon after these events begin to happen.

The race is on, always having to be two steps ahead of her father, Carrie is smart, smarter than her father gives her credit for. From the time she received the SOS call from her sister, Carrie leaves a clue in the shape of a letter which she hopes her friend will discover once she doesn't turn up for their celebration. Inside the letter Carrie is telling her friend Gerry of her possible kidnap and a device, which Gerry is to use to track her and the race is on to get to Carrie.

INDEX

1: The Great Escape

2: The Witness

3: I.D.

4: Hide and Seek

5: Marco

6: The Pendent

7: Science Lab

8: Katakana, the Alien

9: Witness Report

10: "Earthlings of the Surface never see us"

11: Plotting the Escape

12: The Hologram

13: First visit to Surface Earth

14: Following a Trail

15: New Acquaintances

16: “Tender Hooks”

17: Family Reunion

18: Twist of Faith

19: Women’s Power

20: Sector 7

21: Ambush

22: Grand Jury

23: Blue Marco

24: Gifts

25: Re-unification

Appendix: Book 2, Chapter 1

CHAPTER 1

The Great Escape

Geraldine was pacing back and forth. Where the devil was Carrie. Carrie had been with her flat mate all through University. They both studied the same courses, and both had passed with flying colours and now was the time to celebrate before they decided which job opportunities lay before them.

She knew that Carrie had been wanting to travel a bit before deciding to settle down to a job, but Geraldine would need a job to live in her flat. It had been fine when Carrie was helping out with the finances but now that she would be leaving, Geraldine knew she had to find some sort of job; even temporarily, to subsidise until she found her perfect job.

Time was ticking by still no sign of Carrie which was very unusual for her, being the type of person to always be on time for any event no matter how big or small.

Concerned, Geraldine decided to call their friends. They had been planning to meet up to celebrate the occasion. Geraldine was hoping that maybe she had called into see them before coming home and had gotten side-tracked. She picked up her mobile phone and began punching in the telephone numbers.

"Hey, there" a male voice answers. She recognizes the voice, *"Hello Simon. Is Jenny there? I'm calling to see if* Carrie *has called by to see you, as she is extremely late."*

A few seconds later a female voice comes on the line. "What's up Geraldine, thought you and Carrie were meeting us up later?"

"That's why I'm ringing you. She hasn't turned up to the flat, I've tried calling her and no answer on her mobile and that's very unusual for her, I'm really worried!"

"Okay, let me ring around for you. Surely someone will have seen her ...(Pause).... You know, she was a strange girl to be honest. She would disappear for a few hours and then turn up as though nothing out of the ordinary."

"Oh, I didn't know about this," came Geraldine's reply.

"This was before she hooked up with you", Jenny replied.

"Okay well let me know if anyone has seen her and if she does turn up, I will let you know" Geraldine replied with uncertainty in her voice.

Carrie was at this very moment being held against her will. Her father had sent two men to hold onto her until he arrived, but her younger sister Connie was also being held with her. Carrie had managed to hide from her father over the years, mixing with people of her own age. She had changed her name to Carrie and had managed to hide her true identity. For years it had worked but now the game was up.

Carrie knew during her last secret mission to visit her world and to see her youngest sister Constance (Connie) that someone may have seen her and followed. She had escaped her father's clutches many lifetimes ago so it seemed, but now he had found her and although not afraid of him knew the punishments would too severe. Her mother on the other hand was a gentle soul, who also lived in fear of her husband's wrath.

Geraldine still confused, worried, and concerned about Carrie's disappearance, decided to search Carrie's room. Maybe a clue lay there; she had not wanted to pry, but desperate people did desperate things.

Carrie's room was how she remembered it, neat and tidy. She looked around and noticed for the first time an envelope tucked under one of her many ornaments. Going over Geraldine pulled the envelope away from under the said ornament, staring at it she recognized her own name. Carefully she opened the letter and sat down on Carrie's bed to read it.

Dear Geraldine. *("Dear **Geraldine**"?* She's never called me **Geraldine!!!** ... this is serious, this letter is not off to a good start! Geraldine thought to herself.*)*

If your reading this letter now, then you know something has happened to me. Before going out today my sister made contact with me. She never contacts me! The only reason she would, would be because something has happened......... and that that "something" has to do with our father. He may have forced her to make contact with me, to bring me out of hiding. I know you are surprised to hear I have a sister and that I was in hiding. I am sorry, I never confided in you. It is a long story, but I will try to keep this brief.

My sister put herself at risk by reaching out to me. You see, our father is not the type of person that anyone would walk over. The fact that I have not returned, and you are reading this letter, please understand, that I am being held against my will by father and his henchmen and are now forcing me return back to my own world.

(Sister? Henchmen? ... cruel father? ... how did she never confide in me? Not that I could have been of much help ...but **STILL**!?! **Who** or **what** is she? And what exactly does she mean by "Forcing me back to my **OWN** world??? What is she an Alien, hahaha or is she?)

Gerry, my real name is Caroline and I come from a place not of the Earth as you know of but of the Inner Earth.

(hahahaha hahaha, yeah right! What next? **Inner Earth?** What has she been smoking? Hahaha*!)*

I have a younger sister her name is Constance and our mother's name is Rebecca. My father is a tyrant, and many people are afraid of him. Not me! I was planning ahead. During one of his many visits to other sectors within my world, I planned my escape and made my way up to the surface; there were many obstacles in my way, but I managed to escape. My father does not like to be outwitted and he also knows I don't fear him.

(GOSH!!!! She is serious!)

So now down to the most important thing: I need your help! It is my understanding that my sister was forced to contact me and by now I am being held captive by my father's men, and he will be most likely finishing up some business before coming to escort me back to our world.

Recently I have been having a feeling I was being watched but kept shrugging it off oh how I wished I had not. I don't know what father is planning. I know that he will have conjured up some scheme about the sudden return of his daughter. But what I do know is that my sister was very frantic, and I could tell very afraid!

Sitting there Geraldine was finding it hard to take everything in, she returned to reading the letter.

So Gerry, I can only try and be direct to you. Look inside

this envelope. You will find a small tracking device. It is small so you wouldn't 'ave really seen it, but I have enabled it for you. All you need to do is switch the device on at the side and it will lead you to where I am as I have placed the chip inside of me for protection, you will need help, so I suggest calling Simon. You may tell them as much or as little as you feel they should know but I TRUST YOU WITH MY LIFE!

Your friend, *Carrie*

I TRUST YOU WITH MY LIFE! – GULP.

Geraldine looked at the bottom of the envelope and sure enough there it was a small tracking device. She had never seen one before. As soon as she touched it, it began to vibrate and then a very weak signal appeared on the device: a small dot and lines. Just HOW on earth could such a small device like this even have this showing up?

Geraldine rushed to the phone and dialled Simon's number.

"Hello Simon, is Jenny still there."

"Yeah you want her?"

"No!"

"Okay what's up?"

(PAUSE, thinking what to say) "Can you both come over to my place? Carrie has been kidnapped by some men who her father had employed to capture her. It's a long story, but we need to hurry"

Simon began to laugh. *"Hahahaha, that's a good 'n!"*

"Simon!!! Stop laughing!!!! This is serious! She escaped her father's clutches a long time ago and now he has found her, and on his way to take her back home. But she doesn't want that. She wants to live her life the way she wants to."

"Okay, Okay! Keep your hair on! We will be with you in about 15 minutes" and hung up.

Geraldine sat down to re-read the letter, she needed to discuss this with Simon and Jenny and hopefully by showing them Carrie's letter and the device surely, they would be willing to help her or give her the best advice on which way to go out it. She didn't know enough to wonder, if it was much better to contact the police or to find her for themselves, the waiting for Simon and Jenny would be stressful but they are the only people she could really trust, and Carrie's life depended on them.

Still deep in thought Geraldine was brought back to the present by the bell ringing on her door. She opened it to Simon and Jenny and to her amazement, there, standing with them were two of their other friends: Misty and Paul.

"Brought reinforcements in case they are needed" was all Simon said.

"Come in everyone, and I will explain everything to you and welcome Misty and Paul. Glad to have you both onboard hopefully once you all have read Carrie's letter."

So, in saying this, Geraldine gave the letter to Simon who in turn after reading it passed it along until everyone had fully read it and then was passed back to Geraldine.

"Okay everyone, what do you think we should do? Personally, I don't think the police would take this seriously but from what I know about Carrie this is very real and she is in great danger!"

Paul stood up and began pacing the room. He needed to think.

"Misty and myself are both Black Belts and I have connections if we need getaway vehicles. Who here can ride a motorcycle?" asked Paul.

Everyone raised their hands; he sat down and began to look at the tracking device and then pulled out his mobile and phoned the people about the motorbikes. He then proceeded to pull up a map on his phone giving details of where they were and then looking at the device, he calculated that Carrie was in a radius of four to five blocks from Geraldine and Carrie's flat.

He looked back at everyone and said:

"Lads, she is not that far away from here and between us all we can over-power two men hopefully that is all that her father has sent, but we also need weapons for defending ourselves. Geraldine do you have anything we can use for weapons like knives or bats, anything to give us a better advantage?"

Geraldine ran into the kitchen and came out with some knives and a bat, they all looked at her in amazement, she smiled, and produced a taser.

"Good Geraldine and can I ask how in the world you have a taser?" Paul has asked.

She smiled and put her finger to her mouth as to say she wasn't telling and laughed. Paul just shook his head and with a look around at the others motioned for them to proceed out of the door. They would start this journey or adventure together and whichever way this would turn out to be, one thing was for certain, it was going to be better than sitting at home and catching up on his exams.

Silently and in thought they all went out of the flat, and into the elevator. Once they had reached the ground floor level, they piled out and proceeded to go out of the main building door. Paul was first out through the door and once everyone was out on the footpath, Paul put out his hand to Geraldine and asking her to give him the tracker.

Geraldine hesitated at first, then handed it to him. Paul studied it and he reckoned they need to move due North to try to pick up the signal better. Together they followed Paul, who was keeping an eye on the signal as they moved.

At one point the signal seemed to go weaker, so they backtracked to where the signal had been the strongest. Now which way were they to go? Paul signalled for them to stay where they were. He turned to face East to see if the signal would became stronger, he crossed the road keeping the easterly direction, but the signal became weaker, so returned to his companions. They then proceeded West.

Aware, how easy it was to lose the strong signal, they all proceeded cautiously. The signal became stronger and stronger as they walked. Their excitement was tangible ....The signal strength was increasing... they nearly held their breaths, signal continued to increase.... They crossed the road...gone! Gone! "***Sugar Ray Dumplings! Don't you hate that when that happens! I knew it was too good to be true! Sugar! Sugar! Sugar!***" Geraldine surprised herself and the others with her outburst.

"*For goodness sake!*" giving Geraldine a harsh look, " *We all need to backtrack again to where the signal was the strongest and then find out where it started to go weak.*" Paul said more composed.

They found where the signal was the strongest and now, they had to figure out again in which direction they had go to from here: East or West?

Paul decided to move first to his left, and he found the signal was getting stronger. He continued to follow the signal. Looking up he noticed what was some sort of waste land. He beckoned them all to come and they immediately ran over to him.

"*Now this is weird! I can't see anywhere on this vast waste land where they could be hiding but let's move forward again and see what happens.*" Paul is motioning with his arm from left to right, as he is saying this, as to highlight the sheer size of this land waste.

"*Don't forget, Carrie said she comes from Inner Earth. So it would probably be quite logical that there must be some sort of entrance here we just need to find it.*" Said Geraldine.

"*Right! I get it.*" said Paul.

So, they all moved as one Paul using the tracker and everyone looking for anything that would give them the sign of something not right.

Suddenly Paul stopped in his tracks. He was looking down in disbelief. He was looking at something that looked like a manhole cover. 'This can't be right. What would a manhole cover be doing out here?', he thought. 'Impossible! ... Impossible? ... hmmm ... well not all that impossible but was this what they were all looking for?'

Shouting at the rest to come over he knelt down and began looking for any kind of way to open that manhole. He could not find any possible way of doing it. Geraldine came over and said

"Let's all look for something we can use to lever it open."

Everyone went on a search until Simon shouted over that he had found something that could possibly be used to lever up the manhole. He was waving what looked to be a piece of metal.

They all gathered around the manhole cover. Simon produced the metal rod and they all set to work to lever the manhole cover up, it was taking a lot of effort. This was unusual, as they are normally just sort of laying of the manhole, like a saucepan lid on a saucepan.

Eventually they managed to prise it open and peering down Paul noticed why they had such a hard time to loosen it; there was another lever attached to it but with all their hard work it seemed to have loosened it and now was just dangling.

They all started to descend the steps the boys taking the lead and the girls following, they all waited at the bottom to see if anyone had heard them come down, seemingly not. Slowly and as quietly as they could and the boys again taking the main lead, they walked along this path. Suddenly the boys came to a halt and putting their finger up to their lips, indicating to be quiet. Something was up that much the girls knew.

"We can see some sort of light ahead and a bit of activity, we need to move silently and slowly. We don't want to alert whoever is up

there. We don't know what kind of weapons they may have but caution is a must at this time." Paul said.

He moved over to Misty and began talking to her quietly.

"Okay, gather around. Misty and I, as you all know, are Black Belts in self-defence. So we shall move ahead and see what we find. The rest of you must remain here until we let you know the coast is clear. No need for everyone to get caught now, is there!" Said Paul

All agreed and Paul and Misty moved forward, and they could see that the light was getting much stronger. They had no plan of action. They would just take it as it came but one thing was sure: the people ahead would have no idea they were coming.

As Paul and Misty came into view more, they noticed two men guarding two girls. This must be Carrie and her sister Connie. Paul acted immediately on impulse.

"Hi there, my girlfriend and myself seem to be a bit lost. Can you direct us to the way out?"

Both men were startled but regained their composure, looking at the two people moving towards them.

"How did you get here?" Asked the tallest of the men.

"I just told you we came down a manhole and started to walk ... but we seem to have stumbled on something here. What's your game mate and why are you holding them two girls captive? That's what I'd like to know!" came the reply from Paul

"Mind your own business! These two girls have nothing to do with you. So move on, or you will regret it! Buggar off now! Go on! Get ***OUT NOW, OR ELSE*** *...."* came back the reply from the tallest of the men.

Very controlled and not braking eye contact, Paul says: "I think I will make it my business: two men and two young girls just doesn't smell right to me."

Misty was just observing the situation. Waiting for just the right moment. She knew Paul well enough, to tell, when he was working towards something, a plan of some sort. She would look out for his subtle hints pointing towards a possible scenario that would be to their advantage. Slowly moving forward Misty stood in front of the other man and smiled to him. He looked at her as though trying to figure what she was going to do next, but never underestimate Misty. Misty is a fast and precise. Every move is calculated and never misses her target.

Watching Misty from the corner of his eye Paul also moved forward slightly, he then looked towards the two girls.

Shouting over to Misty: *"Hey Misty. Isn't that Carrie over there? What in God's name is she doing here down with these two men?"*

*"**Get a move on!**." shouted the taller of the men, this time with more anger in his voice.*

"It sure is!" replied Misty.

"We are not leaving this place without our classmate Carrie and I think we might as well take the other girl with us; what you think Misty?" asked Paul.

"I SAID GET A MOVE ON!" and moved forward to within a few inches of Pauls face.

Without warning Paul made his move and kickboxed the man sending him off balance. Paul continued to attack with karate chops and he finally went down unconscious. While Paul was busy acting out his self-defence moves, Misty was still facing the other man. He, on the other hand, was stunned by what he had just witnessed. 'How could this whippet take out my partner?' he thought. Misty did not hesitate any longer, she attacked him with her furious karate moves and down he went, like a sack of spuds and unconscious he lay there, too.

Shouting for the others to join them now, all five of them

stood facing Carrie and her sister, they presumed.

"Now what?" asked Simon.

"We need to ask Carrie that I would think." came the reply from Geraldine.

Geraldine moved towards the girls and took the gags off them and untied them. Carrie flung her arms around Geraldine's neck and sobbed. Connie in the meantime was just sitting there taking it all in and watching her sister embracing her friend. She wished she had friends like that but was not envious.

Geraldine then turned towards Connie and embraced her, asking her if she too were okay. Connie could not believe it. This Surface Earth human was hugging her as if they had known each other for years. This was something she could live with.

CHAPTER 2

The Witness

Geraldine walked towards the others and introduced Connie to them. Connie didn't know what to do. She just stared at them all puzzled, until Carrie came and placed her arm around her shoulders to comfort her. *"They are my Earth-Friends. Now they are yours, too"*, Carrie said with a smile on her face.

Connie turned to face Carrie and handed her a pendant, that had belonged to their mother. '*Why would Connie be now presenting it to me*?' Carrie thought. She looked into Connie's eyes and realized something must have happened. Carrie in turn showed Connie a similar pendant; this too, had belonged to their mother.

With a questioning look, Carrie scanned Connie's face for an explanation to what had happened. She had not had the chance to talk to Connie as they had both been gagged and hands and feet tied.

Geraldine motioned to the others to move slightly away, she realized that Connie needed to talk to her sister in private. Whatever was going on Carrie would let them know as soon as Connie had told her what was going on.

"Carrie, I need to tell you our mother is dead. I was out doing chores in the back when I heard father shouting. Then just complete silence. I was scared of father as you know, his temper is not normal! I went into the house, only to see mother was lying on the floor, and from a deep gash on her head blood was gushing. I went over to her. I was scared. I felt helpless. So much blood....oh Carrie, it was

*awful. Mother, with her dying breath told me to go looking for you and tell you that you needed to look after me, and then told me to take her pendant off her which I did and told me to give it to you. She also told me that there was also another pendant... the same one... in the drawer(she pointed to it) and that I must take it with me. As I was kneeling down beside her, father came in and came over to mother but by then it was too late. He showed no emotions, asked me no questions and bellowed out: "**I KNOW WHO HAS DONE THIS! IT WAS YOUR SISTER THAT'S WHO!**"*

I knew full well though that it was father, but how could I possibly prove it, who would take the word of a child against that of her father who had great influence? I knew then that I had to carry out mother's wishes and got up and walked away with fathers voice in my ear where did I think I was going, I totally ignored him and walked out and into my room. Sitting on my bed I started to think and plot a way out of here. I was re-playing everything over and over in my head. I had heard father scream, well yelling, before-hand, which was followed by silence. See, I knew that father would never take the blame. I knew that he would put the blame on someone else and would either direct it towards myself or you but why you I couldn't fathom. But then, I think maybe he knew that you had been earlier that day to visit mother on one of your secret visits (which never included you seeing father) and I think he had found out."

Carrie looked at her sister in shock. Her thoughts started to race... '*What was she on about? She had only seen mother yesterday and she was fine. They always kept their visits secret, because if father knew about this, he would stop her from returning back up to the surface. During all her visits to see her mother she had always been scared in case father found out, and seemly now he had and extracted his revenge in such a way that it now denied them of their mother.*'

Carrie and Connie both broke down in tears now the shock of the burden had been told, Connie handed Carrie the pendant her mother had insisted that Carrie should have and immediately put it around her neck. They walked over to the group who had been watching with interest.

"Connie has just informed me that Mother is dead, and that father has killed our mother. Whether accidently or with intent is unknown. The fact is, however, we can now not go back to our home but must now move up on to the surface and hope that we can both learn to live together."

Shock and horror is written all over their faces. What the devil was going on? Their father is now a murderer??? What a turn of events, but they also knew they needed to get away as soon as possible. Their father will surely be on his way to pick up his children and when he finds them gone, his anger will hold no bounds.

Paul decided the best thing to do was that he went ahead and telephoned his friends to come with the motor bikes so that they can get away as fast as possible, if these henchmen where anything to go by it would be quite obvious that their father would have some sort of weapon and they didn't want to wait around to witness whatever he would do.

Paul reached the man-hole cover, edged it to one side, climbed up and phoned his friend...told him that they needed the motorbikes ASAP and given the rendezvous point.

The others started to move. They had heard some voices in the distance coming up the tunnel. They more or less had to run the rest of the way to the manhole. One by one they climbed to the surface, each one looking around nervously and when the last one had climbed out , they replaced the lid.

"I need to speak to Paul and Misty on their own," said Carrie.

Going over to the two she now trusted with her life, she began telling them that they too, where also now in great danger. She went on explaining these henchmen had photographic memories and they would also use photo recognition to trace them.

"So what your saying is that they will also come after us because they may think we know where you are or maybe punish us both for helping you escape??? What about the rest? Oh yeah. They didn't actually see them. Only myself and Misty."

"Yes, that is exactly what I am saying. The others were not visible to them whereas you both were! They don't even know if Simon and Jenny were here." replied Carrie.

"Absolutely great! Just FAAAAN-BLOOMING-TASTIC! We are now in danger, too, but I have my exams to finish tomorrow as does Misty. And then we can disappear; we just need these exams done to be able to go on with our future." Paul said and you could see the tension and frustration in his face.

"Okay, okay.... I do understand. I also have to get the results from my exams, and I am hoping that by going to Simon and Jennies apartment that I can get the results of my exams and hopefully get them to send my diplomas to me." replied Carrie.

"Geraldine has finished all of hers and she is also waiting her results." Said Carrie

"So what's the best option? What shall we do?" asked Misty, *"Either we do our exams tomorrow or we skip them and destroy our future, and I for one certainly want to finish my exams to be able to get the rest of my results, I have earned my diploma as has Paul."*

"Let us talk this over with the others first and go from there."

They walked over to the others just as the motorbikes came into view, they all ran towards the bikes and each rider mounted with their passengers.

"So where do we all go," asked Geraldine.

"Simon and Jennies place. We need to discuss things and it is going to be the safest place for everyone, until we can figure things out." Carrie said.

They all set of, Connie, who had never sat on one of those 2-wheeled vehicles, was clinging on for dear life behind Paul, she had been instructed to go with Paul as being the most experienced of all.

Within fifteen minutes they were all outside of Simons apartment the bikes were stored in the garage below out of sight, they were not taking any chances.

In Simons apartment refreshments where handed out, Connie didn't know what to make of the coke she had been given but decided she would give it a try, taking her first sip she was surprised how tasty it was and drank some more. Carrie was sitting watching her sister and smiling. There was only three years difference between them, but Connie had never experienced anything other than the life below in Inner Earth.

"Okay everyone listen up, Carrie has been informing me that because Misty and myself went and attacked them henchmen, our lives are possibly in danger now. The thing being both of us have our last exams tomorrow and then after that we need to be able to wait until our results come through.
If what Carrie tells me is right, her father will not immediately come up to the surface he will go back and bring reinforcements, presuming he has managed to convince others that his wife's murder is no other than his oldest daughter." Paul said, trying not to sound fearful.

"Both Connie and myself have no right to put your lives in danger and I want to thank you from the bottom of my heart for rescuing us. What I need to do is talk this over with Connie, but I think our best option here is to move States once I get my results through and my diploma. I can get myself a position and provide for myself and Connie, I want Connie to have a stable life without fear and I am going to start by looking for the largest city to hide in, and then need to get her enrolled in a school." Carrie sounded as if she had it all already worked out.

"So, what your suggesting is moving away altogether, with no friends to rely on.... that is the craziest thing I've ever heard." said Geraldine.

"I need to keep Connie and myself safe. Father will never rest until he has us both back in Inner Earth, and me tried for murder, this will not happen. For one thing we need to think this through, eventually I will have to return but I want it on my terms, and I want to be able to prove my innocence." Carrie said with firmness in her voice.

Everyone settled down and discussions began. Carrie told Connie to go rest up in one of the spare bedrooms. The discussions went on into late hours and the only conclusion that came was that Carrie and Connie must leave by first light tomorrow. Tickets to be bought, no airplane, everything would need to be via public transport, changing where necessary. They had decided that Carrie would pick the place, buy the necessary tickets but final destination would never be disclosed to any of them. She would only contactable via telephone or email. And this too, maybe should be coded and possibly encrypted, for who knows what technology they have in Inner Earth, to infiltrate emails. Mobile phones and numbers would be changed on an irregular bases, well Carrie's cell phone would have to be. They agreed to a code for now, which also would be changed frequently. Only Carrie would keep their numbers written down separately in a diary like book. This was the only way to keep everyone safe.

Once everyone had agreed on Carrie and Connie's next move, the next topic to be discussed was Paul and Misty: they needed to go for their exams the following day, then once done they would go to somewhere safe, Paul had many friends as did Misty one of them would hide them until they figured out their next move. But they also thought they may need to move to another State, and not where Carrie or Connie were. And this could be tricky, as nobody would know, where Carrie and Connie would have moved to. So they agreed on directions: Pacific, Atlantic, Midlands, Southern or Northern States.

Geraldine cried, she was going to lose her friends. Simon and Jenny told her that they would always be there for her and her sister, no matter what.

It was getting late and Geraldine decided she need to go back to her own apartment. She needed a shower and clean clothes. She had promised Carrie she would pack her clothes and books for her and bring them over to Simon's first thing in the morning by taxi.

Geraldine moved towards the door and bade goodnight to everyone and left the apartment. She had already called for a taxi as she hated being out alone at night.

Everyone else in the flat settled down, Simon and Jenny shared one bed and Paul and Misty the other, nothing unusual to that they had slept together before. Carrie went to where her sister was only to find her fast asleep, she lay down next to her and fell asleep.

Geraldine arrived at her home, she was about to get out of the taxi when she noticed what looked like flashlights going off in the apartment, leaning over to the taxi driver she pointed up towards her apartment, he looked up and then picked up his phone and dialled the police.

Coming off the phone he told her the police were on their way and to stay in the taxi, the taxi driver called into the office explained the position and turned off his meter. They waited. Now they could hear police sirens coming up the street...

The lights in the flat seemed to go off, and she watched as two men came out of the entrance straight into the arms of the Law, Geraldine got out of the taxi and told the officers that these men did not live in this block and suspected them to be the ones inside of her apartment. The two men glared at Geraldine and were escorted into the cars. Geraldine sighed in relief, turned to pay the taxi driver thanked him for his help and started to go towards the entrance when a policewoman stopped her and told her that she would be escorting her up to the apartment to make sure nobody was still in it. They went up in the lift to the apartment....upon entering the apartment it was such a mess... things thrown all over the place.... she rushed into Carrie's bedroom... everything was scattered.... her clothes in a heap on the bed....books pulled from shelves, some open, desk drawers pulled out.... walking from there to her own bedroom, the same thing. Her heart sank. Thank God, the Police Officer was with her and recorded everything. But the question was: *did them thugs find what they were looking for?* She thanked the policewoman for having escorted her to the apartment and for having witnessed the state of the apartment.

Lodged the crime report – because of the Landlord, made it all official. The Officer suggested she would stay and take some pictures of the apartment and record her findings and if Geraldine wanted, take this time to freshen up. Geraldine went into the bathroom and ran the shower. *"WHAT A DAY THIS TURNED OUT TO BE, BUT WHAT NEXT???"* she said to herself out loud in the shower. After drying herself, getting into her PJs, hair still wrapped in the towel, she called Simon. It took a bit for the receiver to pick up, a yawning Simon asked *"...who is this? ..."* He recognized Geraldine's voice, he sat upright in bed and was wideawake.

Simon: *"What's happened?"*

Geraldine: *"I arrived home, saw lights on in the apartment so called the police, two men were arrested and now in police custody, a policewoman escorted me up to my apartment, recorded every, filed the complaint, she's still here, but I now don't trust anyone hence in bathroom with shower running and calling you."*

Simon: *"Okay here's what I want you to do, collect up Carrie's clothes and yours, looks like you're not even safe, just collect what* *you can, I will wake up Paul and see if we can get some muscle over there to help you pack up everything you need and get you back here."*

Geraldine: *"Okay but what about the policewoman outside, how do I explain things to her, she will ask questions if I start to pack up."*

Simon: *"Tell her you don't think anything is missing until you get things back into place and that you will contact the police department should anything be missing, because they have caught the intruders they won't send in the forensic team."*

Finishing her call with Simon, Geraldine went into the room and told the policewoman she would get things straight and see if anything is missing and if there is, she will contact the police department. Nodding, the policewoman opened the door and let herself out of the apartment.

Geraldine scrambled around the bedrooms, packing all of Carrie's clothes, books, and anything else she could think of. Then going into her own bedroom she packed her clothes, books, and other sentimental things. Once done she just sat and waited. Looking around at what she had packed up, there wasn't that much left; the apartment had come furnished so the only things that she had was now all packed away as was Carrie's. Looking around the apartment she looked to see if she had missed anything, suddenly remembering the bathroom she rushed in and put both hers and Carries toiletries into separate bags and put them beside the rest of the stuff.

What seemed ages but was like only 15 minutes later the intercom went, and she breathed a sigh of relief when she heard Simons brother Arthur come onto the intercom. She buzzed for it to let him in and standing with the apartment door open she let him and two of his buddies in, they looked at all the stuff and knew this person was not coming back.

So between them they carried the stuff down and into the van, and once everything was packed, Arthur led her over to another vehicle and told her to get in, looking towards the van, she wondered what was going on.

"What's happening?" asked Geraldine.

"Well just in case anyone is still out there and decides to follow us we go separate ways and then we see which of us has a tail, I suspect there might just be someone watching you, hoping you lead them to your friend, yes Simon told me as much as he could without revealing too much, I trust my brother's judgement and we always help each other out." Arthur said with a serious look on his face.

Thirty minutes later they all pulled up in the street opposite Simons house, there had been no sign of a trail, maybe the two men had been the only ones, but taking no chances.

Geraldine got out of the car and went to Simon's apartment block's front door, rang his doorbell the door opened and both herself, Arthur and his two friends went up to the apartment.

When they entered the apartment everyone was awake, even Connie, it looked like they had all been in conference as though deciding the best course of action now.

"Hi, Geraldine, seems you stumbled onto something tonight and just got away by the skin of your teeth, well done on calling the cops, at least they should be locked up in jail now and know that you can't just go into someone's home." said Paul, sounding relieved but also showing concern.

Arthur went over to the fridge and helped himself to a beer, giving his two mates one each.

"Okay Bro, so what you going to do now? Seems they are onto you all and I think everyone of you should get out of town so to speak. And yes, I know Paul and Misty still have one last set of exams, ...so how about this we escort Paul and Misty to school wait and then drive them back here then everyone is safe for tomorrow at least." suggested Arthur.

"Well only problem with that...." came back Paul, *"...the cam-*

pus is big, and they could find us before you do."

"No problems there, see here, these two they are sitting their own exams tomorrow next door to yours and at the same time. So I suggest once finished you all meet outside of the exam room and make your way over to the car, I will be sitting waiting and watching for any strange vehicles or men." said Arthur, hoping he didn't sound too fatherly.

Simon: *"So that sounds perfect to me, don't you think, Paul? I know you have your martial arts, but what if they send more than two men, how are you and Misty going to take on that many?"*

Paul: *"Okay we do it Arthur's way, but what's after that? Where does everyone go to? Either we all go on the run so to speak or we don't. Personally, I could do with a change of scenery, Simon and Jenny are safe nobody knows they exist."*

Everyone nodded again in agreement, Arthur left with his two mates, and told Paul and Misty they would be fine.

Paul looked at Arthur and deep down he hoped he was right.

CHAPTER 3

I.D.

The following morning both Paul and Misty left the apartment, they looked around as they left, making sure that there was nobody following them. They crossed the road and got into Paul's car and drove to the University Campus. Parking up, they started to look around again, seeing nobody there they started towards the University's main door, when Arthur and his two friends caught up with them nearly frightening the life out of Misty.

They all proceeded towards the main entrance and each went into their separate exam rooms, the exams were much harder than Paul thought, he should have been studying yesterday but he went through the paper, looking over to Misty, he knew she was also miles away. They both finished their papers and when the exam teacher said: "**STOP!**" they knew that was the end of the exams, he went onto say that their exams results will be published on the University website in eight weeks, time.

'*Phew*' thought Paul, '*that's all finished now and all we need to do is wait for the results*.' The fact that they would be published online, was a new thing for the University, instead of having the halls packed with students awaiting their final results. '*PERFECT!*'

Stepping out of the exam room, Paul and Misty looked around for the two friends of Arthur, they had not come out of the room yet! They hoped they would not be too long as they were getting nervous waiting, although the halls were full of students and they knew strangers would stand out nevertheless they were anxious.

Finally, a few minutes later the chaps came out and they all trotted towards Paul's car. Before they even got a chance to open-up the car, Arthur came running over: *"Hang fire mate, two men where snooping around. I saw them earlier waiting around, I think you've been "clocked" as you left your car. They sort of pulled out a device and I think it may be like a facial recognition device. So, you're nabbed!"*
"Gavin! Have a look under the car in case they have put some sort of tracking device on it. If you can't see any then Paul is safe, only thing I do suggest is, we will follow you back to your own digs and hang around. You need to get packing and then the chase is on We will have to do a 'zig zag' and hopefully not leave a trail to Simons." said Arthur.

So saying Paul made a beeline for his apartment and ran upstairs leaving Misty in the car. Then needed to go to her place as well to pick up her things, he left her in the car to go over to Arthur to explain it all. Paul opened the door to his apartment, packed all his clothes and any other personal possessions he put them into the lift and got in himself and down he went, the lift door opened and lo and behold there stood Arthur ready to give him a hand.

"Your girlfriend tells me she has to go to her place to pack her belonging up, is that right? Thought you two lived together. She tells me it is just a block away. So let's get going. The sooner we have you safe and sound the better." Arthur said.

"Yeah that's right, she does live in with some housemates, who aren't actually going to be very happy, she is leaving, but hey, that's life." Paul replied.

So off they all went again to Misty's flat. Paul went up with her to help her and try to explain to her flatmates her sudden leaving. The simplest option was to say, she was moving in with Paul. Arthur had agreed to watch his car whilst he helped Misty pack up. Twenty minutes later a beaming Misty descends out of the main door and they both get into Paul's car; Arthur goes over to his and they all move off again; watching out for any tails. They never saw any so with hope against odds they had gotten away.

Arriving at Simon's: he was standing at the entrance to the garage and beckoned them all to enter, they did so, and he closed the garage door. They all went up to Simon's apartment and the gang were all there waiting to see what had transpired. Accordingly Paul gave them the details and they all sighed with relief that every one of them was safe and sound. They all gathered around the table and started to discuss what to do next. It had become obvious to everyone that not only were Paul and Misty not safe, but neither was Geraldine.

Geraldine: *"Okay because of the state of affairs, Carrie and Connie have decided they need to put as much distance from here as possible. They are looking towards Washington DC. There are three ways of getting there: 1) by train which will take 3 hrs 6mins 2) by bus and that will take 4hrs 37mins or 3) flying that takes 2hr 49 mins. We have ruled out both the train and the flying and think the best possible route for Carrie and Connie is by bus. Although it is the longest route, we can justify that the longest route is the best, this gives them both time to adjust to each other and talk."*

Paul: *"What about the rest of us?"*

Misty: *" We also need to leave town for at least the time being. I've always fancied travelling. So how about it Carrie and Connie, want some company? And hey, Geraldine, why don't you join us? We can all chip in for the digs and share. This way we will be able to support each other until such time we can come back here."*

Carrie: *"Sounds fine by me. Let's go on a journey together, plus I need to search for the right school for Connie, but what about iden-*

tity papers? You lot have them, Connie and I don't, for travelling that is."

Arthur: *"Taken care of! Spoken to my mate.... should be here any minute with ID papers, social security and everything you need to make you legit!"*

Everyone gasped. How on earth had he come up with this lot, they all looked towards Simon who had gone a lovely shade of red.

Simon: *"Well.... since they came from where they did it was obvious, they don't have any sort of ID to be able to move around, so I called Arthur late last night. All he needs now is a photo of the girls and hey presto it's done."*

He went into the bedroom came back with a digital camera, took a photo of Carrie first and then Connie, he then handed the USB stick over to his brother and Arthur left immediately promising to return as soon as possible, but looking like they all had to stay put for another night anyways.

Paul: *"We need to check the timetables and try to get the earlies bus out of town, the quicker we are away the better I feel."*

Carrie: *"I am so deeply sorry, that I have dragged you all into this. It was never my intention. I would have waited for my results and then moved away without having to burden any of you with my problems. There is another entrance to Inner Earth. But for the time being I will hold fire before I let you all know. I need to make sure that entrance hasn't been used in a long time. And all I do know is that it is somewhere in Washington."*

Simon was busy online checking out the timetable and found that they needed to get to Ferry Street, Newark, New Jersey which was in the front of Peter Francisco Park and that it was leaving at 10.30 a.m., just the right time. He then decided he would look for temporary accommodation and found on apartment that would accommodate up to six people, not costly. Now he need to google the area to see how safe it was. After researching the area further on Google, he found it was in a good area uptown and very safe area. It seemed that it was an area where students lived so they should all be safe among other young people.

Carrie had just reached her 21st birthday; her sister Connie was coming up to 18 years of age and still needed some sort of education to be able to acquire a job. Carrie was also googling but for Universities that she thought suitable for her sister and that only required an entrance exam to get in. She thought she may have found one. All she needs to do now was acquire the right entry qualifications to get her in, maybe Simon's brothers contacts could help.

Carrie: *"Simon, does your brother's contacts also do entry papers to get into a University? As I think we may need the for Connie."*

Simon: *"Well, how did you acquire yours?"*

Carrie: *"Simple. I attended a normal school got qualifications for the entry criteria, but Connie hasn't been to school here and so needs those kinds of documentation. My sister is highly qualified in her own right. She has a great mathematical mind as well as technology skills."*

Simon: *"Well why not find her a part-time job and let her decide whether she wishes to go to Uni or not, don't force her. You know the study ethics involved."*

Connie: *"May I speak? Firstly I don't want to go to any University or School or whatever you call it here. What I would like to do as Simon says, is acquire a small part-time job whatever that entails, find my feet, and go from there. I've had enough of people trying to control my life. Mother, she was not pushing but father was, and I hated him for it. He wouldn't let me be myself. Here I can be the person I want to be."*

Carrie stood there sort of in shock, but she did understand

where her sister was coming from. She wanted to enjoy her freedom. Get used to being on the "Surface" among Earth people... the rest can follow... she would make up her own mind. Connie was as strong headed as she was.

Evening came everyone settled down for the night and dreamt of what was to come. They all slept on tender hooks, waking up at the slightest of noises.

Morning finally came they all got up and had breakfast everyone was packed ready and it was only 8.30am. Arthur had phoned that morning waking up Simon, telling him all the paperwork was done. It had been a rush job and his mate was only charging for the I.D. and the rest was free, and he would take care of that cost. He said he would be arriving in half an hour and had the cars to take them to the bus station ready for the journey.

They all sat around waiting, the half hour seemed to drag on but eventually the intercom sounded, Simon went over to it. His brother was waiting downstairs, and for the rest of the journey, he had all the necessary paperwork for Carrie and her sister Connie.

One by one, Connie, Carrie went down first, then Geraldine and Misty. Paul was the last to go down, Simon and Jenny remained inside the apartment block they did not want to be seen. They all got their luggage stored in the three cars, and once everyone was in, they set of for Newark Bus Station giving them plenty of time to get their tickets and board.

They arrived at the bus terminal in plenty of time. They all bought their tickets. All paying cash, so as not to leave a money trail. Once they had bought their tickets they headed over to where the bus was parked up, they all boarded, and each of them thanked Arthur and his friends.

The bus left exactly on time at 10.30am and the new journey of their lives had begun. They hoped that this journey would bring them more happiness than what they had all left behind. Each had money that they knew they would need to pool together to pay the initial deposit for a place, and for food until they could get themselves jobs.

CHAPTER 4

Hide and Seek

Tired and hungry they all arrived at the Union Station Bus Terminal in the District of Columbia Washington. They need to find a place to rest and clean up and see where they go from there. They needed to find accommodation first and foremost; either they find a place to rest for the night or they find an apartment for them all it was a simple as that.

Paul bought a paper and started to go through the list of accommodations and he seemed to have found one, so he dialled the number and asked if the advertised apartment was still for rent and what did it include like furniture etc and was it big enough for five students to live in.

Smiling as he came of the phone: "Well, we may just have hit lucky. I spoke to a lady on the phone and the apartment is about five blocks away from where we are now, so let's head out and hail two taxis and make our way there, apparently all she needs is one month's rent in advance."

Arriving at the apartment block they were sort of looking at it and thinking they had landed on their feet they just hoped that the inside of the apartment lived up to the same as the front. Paul rang the bell, and a middle-aged woman answered the door, she beckoned them to enter and they came in with their luggage in tow.

"Good afternoon. These are my friends and one of who is my fiancé. We are just looking for an apartment and when we spoke on the phone you said you had one for rent on the first floor." said Paul

She led the way to the lift and walked in with Paul and Misty. The others joined in with their luggage in tow. Going up in the lift Paul had the strongest feeling that they had landed right on their feet. Opening the door to the apartment, one by one they all entered. It was lovely. Seemed as though newly decorated as well, they had landed on their feet. They looked at each other, smiling. Each knowing they had come to the right place.

So the lady asked Paul to come with her and he followed her back downstairs. She informed him that she held him responsible for the upkeep of the apartment and he had to sign a 3 months lease on it, which in all fairness was fine by Paul, he reckoned they would be staying here for that length of time anyways. The lady explained that she only gave the three-monthly lease until she was sure that they would pay for it and no damages. Her other statement was that no late-night parties were allowed and only those occupying the apartment were allowed inside. Any other people she needed to know about as she had all her other tenants to think about.

Paul assured her that this would be fine by him and his friends, they were not the partying type. She then proceeded to give him four sets of keys; each set let them in through the front door and the apartment. Paul handed her the right monthly rent in advance and proceeded towards the lift.

Paul entered the apartment and gave them the same instructions the old lady had given to him and the duration of the lease. They all agreed this was ample enough time to find the right accommodation to suit all their needs but in the meantime this would do they had been incredibly lucky indeed.

Paul sat down at the table and bringing out his phone dialled the number Arthur had given him, after a few rings Arthur answered the phone he told Arthur they had all arrived safely at their destination and found an adequate apartment until they found other accommodation and that they would now be on the hunt for jobs.

Arthur: *"Great to hear from you Paul, I will pass on the message to Simon and Jenny. So, you managed to secure an apartment, well done to you all! Simon was a bit worried just in case you were followed but it seems at the moment you haven't been."*

Paul: *"Any sign of anything you can reach me at this number, it's one of them pay as you go phones, so not traceable."*

Arthur: *"I personally think you should only use disposables for the time being and try to keep away from the internet at least until things sort of die down.*

Paul: *"Impossible ... we need to access our results and get our diplomas, because without them then we are stuck in a jam."*

Arthur: *"Okay, well I suggest using an internet café and different ones all the time, once you are sure your results are through get yourselves a P.O. Box number and get them sent to that."*

Paul: *"Never thought of that, maybe your right.... at least if it goes to the P.O. Box number, we can watch out for anything suspicious before we collect it."*

Arthur: *"Isn't this like the movies, like spy ones?"*

Paul: *"Giggle, yah I guess, but no not really. I don't like to be on the receiving end of it, and what has to be had to be...."*

They all scanned the newspaper in the job sector they were looking for jobs to go with their studies even though they didn't actually have their diplomas, yet they could still apply for the relevant jobs, many firms did take on junior roles until such time your qualifications came through. Carrie looked down the list of jobs and spotted an advertisement that just may be suiting her. There was a telephone number to call, it was working in a large corporation in the Research and Science field. She met the criteria but until she got her diploma through, but would they accept her?

They all egged her on to telephone for the job. In the end she did that and after about ten minutes of talking she came of the phone with a smile.

Carrie: *"There is a junior position going in the research laboratory that they think I could be suitable for. They would need to interview me and, on the understanding that they would want references they would like to see me tomorrow morning at 11.30 am. "* You could hear her excitement but also concern: *"Where am I going to get references from at such short notice? Normally they look for one from your University and from someone who has known you for years."*

Misty: *"Now that is easy. All you have to do is email your Professor, explain you have the opportunity to acquire a job. Ask him then if he could possibly give you a reference and if so, that you would put him down as the first reference."*

Carrie knew this was a risk, but one, she was prepared to take. She knew that it would be far safer for her to use her 'Pay-as-you-go' disposable cell phone, to phone the Uni and speak to her Professor personally.

So Carrie went over to her backpack and picked up her mobile phone and began dialling the number for the main reception of the University. Once she was through, she asked to speak to Professor Richards and explaining the reason, she was then put through to his office.

Carrie: *"Sorry to disturb you, Professor Richards. I would like to know if you could possibly give me a reference as I need one for the job I am applying for and they would need to have a name for a reference."*

Professor Richards: *"Sure just tell them to contact me and I will gladly give them a reference. And Carrie, while I have you on the phone, I was wanting to talk to you. A man came to me today and asking for your whereabouts, didn't seem a nice character to be honest. He was asking if I had heard from yourself. Of course, I hadn't, and he seemed satisfied and asked if I heard from you to please let him* *know. Apparently, it seems he is your father." Came the* reply.

Carrie: *"Oh my goodness, please can you not tell him of my contacting yourself and not to let him know where I am! He is a bully and has made my life hell. This is why I have actually moved away from Jersey to get as far away from him as possible."*

Professor Richards: *"Of course! I would never divulge your whereabouts of which at this present time I know not where you are, but I daresay that your new employers will be contacting me and then I will probably know exactly where you are."*

Carrie: *"I beg you please, he can be very persuasive in getting what he wants. He more or less will not take no for an answer."*

Professor Richards: *"Wherever you are he won't hear it from me, in fact I would prefer if your new employers used my own personal email account that way it isn't going through the school account."*

Carrie: *"Thank you Sir! I won't forget this! I will also eventually need my diploma results which I know will be posted on the University Website. I will if successful send for my diplomas."*

Coming of the phone she told the others that her father had actually been enquiring about her whereabouts, and that Prof Richards didn't know, which at that time, he didn't! He has promised if these prospective employers accept me that they have permission to email him to his own personal email account for a reference.

"Now that only leaves one more reference to acquire," Carrie said.

"Why not get Simon to ask your old boss to see if she will give you a reference? He can then pick it up by hand and post it to our Registered Post Box at the Post Office." replied Paul.

"Good idea!" said Carrie.

The others were still scanning the jobs sector when Geraldine piped up. She had found a job that suited her 'to the tea'. Then Misty said she may have just found a position and that only left Paul. He couldn't find anything, maybe there will be something in the late evening papers.

Geraldine and Misty phone up their prospective employers and each had acquired an interview for the following day in the afternoon.

Connie was sitting still, not even looking at the papers. She was too interested in what was going on outside, she was fascinated by the flowing of the traffic and the sirens from the Police cars. It was so different from Inner Earth but was exciting. She was looking forward to embracing this new world she had found herself in. Connie knew she would miss the companionship of her friends from Inner Earth. They had been her salvation when her father was in one of his moods...

Paul got up and telling everyone he was going out to get food and more importantly the evening papers he needed to find work.

CHAPTER 5

Marco

Paul walked along the street. He had put up his hood; he was still nervous in one sense since Carrie had mentioned facial recognition. As he kept going and watching for hidden cameras on street corners, over retail outlets and the likes, he was wondering if he would ever get used to ducking and diving, living in fear.... there had to come a time when he would have to learn to trust in himself and his capabilities in his martial arts.

In in thoughts as he is going down this street, he suddenly notices a martial arts club. Curiosity got the better of him, so he walked over and started reading the information in the window. Paul was impressed. '*This is just the right place for me*' he thought, '*and once I secure a job this is where I'll go to keep up with my marital arts*'.

He was still studying the noticeboard when a man came out and asked him if he was interested in joining. Paul explained briefly that he was knew in town and that he was looking for a job first before he could continue with his martial arts.

The man's curiosity took the better of him. "You already do martial arts? In what capacity have you studied and what is your current level?" Paul explained he was a black belt in karate, and black belt in kick boxing and he had been studying to become a Master/Teacher within his martial arts. He had also been attending Uni. He wanted to have other qualifications to fall back on.

"Come with me let me see what you can do. My name is Marco and

I own this club"

So, doing as Marco asked, he followed him into the club. He was shown to a locker, was handed training outfit to get changed into, and then to join Marco inside. He entered the training hall and looked around. Marco and Paul were alone. He told Paul to show him what he was made of and so he did. Marco was impressed....*'maybe this is what he has been looking for?'* Marco had been planning to advertise the vacancy for a martial arts instructor, but it seemed he had found what he was looking for.

"Can you come back tomorrow morning with all your credentials proving what degree you are at in Karate and Kick Boxing. If you are who I think you are I would like to offer you a permanent position as an instructor." Said Marco.

'***WOW****! Was this really happening? he had only walked out of the apartment to go pick up a newspaper to scour for job vacancies and now it looked like he possibly had one all he needed to do was show his credentials.'* Paul thought to himself.

"Yes! Sure I can call back first thing tomorrow and bring them to you to show you. Can I ask you one thing, where is the nearest store? I need to get some supplies for me and my friends seeing we have only just moved here." Said Paul. *"Sure. There is a store about 100 yards up the road, it sells just about everything there is. You should find exactly what you need to see you over until tomorrow. Your friends can then go to the larger mall a short bus ride from here."* Marco said.

So, it now looked like all of their lives were settled all accept Connie that was, they had to find something for her but what? Maybe a part time job in a shop where she wouldn't be under scrutiny. Yes things where starting to come together. Strange how Life throws you a curve ball, but maybe their lives are entwined together. In martial arts we are taught about karma and life paths; how some need to cross your path, forcing you to take a direction, you otherwise wouldn't have. Or sometimes enter your presence and those of others, drawing you all closer together. And right now, only together, and under these circumstances they could work on the safety and security for all involved.

Paul entered the apartment half an hour later to be greeted by anxious eyes. He smiled at them all. No, not smiling, he was grinning like a Cheshire cat! They all looked at him wondering what had happened. They thought he had gotten lost or something had happened, Paul seemed to have been gone for ages, considering he was only getting the Evening Papers and a bite to eat.

"Were have you been?!? I've been so worried about you! You have taken ages to come back and the shop is only up the road so don't give any excuses! " Misty said with real concern in her voice.

"I guess, you don't want to hear my good news then, or do you?" asked Paul

This got their attention. They were all ears and eager for Paul to continue. But, instead, he marched into the kitchen and began emptying the bags. He was making them wait and Carrie could see Misty was ready to hit him. " *Okay, I'm all ears! Come on then, let's all hear your good news!"* came from Carrie.

"Okay. I have acquired myself a job and all I need to do is show my martial arts certifications to prove that I have attained my qualifications and the job is mine as a Trainer in Martial Arts." Paul said, trying to contain his true excitement.

They all looked stunned; more so Misty: *"How the devil did that happened? You only went to the shop!"* she went over to him and asked him to tell them all.

"Right, I was walking down towards the shops when I spotted the Martial Arts Club. Well and you know me Misty, I can't help but take a look. Anyways, to shorten a long story, the man who owns the club asked me if I wanted to join up as a member. I told him that I was

looking for a job first but once I had I wanted to continue my martial arts training. He then asked me what I had, and I told him Black Belt in both Karate and Kick Boxing and he seemed impressed. Anyways, he told me to come inside and I had to show him what I was made of; hence how it took me so long to come back with groceries. He was so impressed he offered me a full-time job as a martial arts teacher. He would be guiding me. I would be learning under him and he reckons within a few months I will gain my Marital Arts Teaching Certification through him. In other words, he is training me to become a teacher." Paul explained, grinning from ear to ear.

"Wow that is fantastic, I can't believe you have gotten the job of your dreams. They say, dreams can come true and I think we are all going to be living our dreams, only person now who needs help is Connie." Misty exclaimed.

Carrie had been thinking on the same lines. She had seen a part time job as a junior shop assistant in a shop dealing with clothing and she knew Connie loved clothes. Carrie decided that Connie needed to apply for the job. But there was only a small problem, she had was no work experience. The job's ad had said "junior", so maybe they would be some training on the job. She picked up her phone and dialled the number changing her voice pattern to be more like Connie's. She asked about the job and they said they would interview her tomorrow. Carrie explained acting as Connie, she didn't have any experience and they told Carrie that she would be trained; Connie that is.

Coming off the phone she looked at Connie and to her amazement her sister smiled and laughed for the first time since this journey had started. It was lovely to hear her laughing, she ran over to Carrie and hugged her tight.

"That job will be simply perfect for me, don't you think? You know how I love clothes and Earthling clothes I am really excited about seeing and hopefully I can buy some once I have money to do so." Connie said, sounding really happy.

They were all hungry, so Geraldine cooked them all a meal, they put on the TV and sat back and watched a good movie. It had been a long but exciting day and they decided to have an early night because everyone had to be fresh for tomorrow.

Connie looked at Carrie and then down at her own clothes. Carrie looked at her. They were actually the same build, so Carrie led her to her wardrobe and chose a beautiful flowery dress and shoes and bag, they looked lovely on Connie. Connie ready for her interview. Connie was nervous, but Carrie had promised she would be there for her at her interview.

Morning came and went they all went to their relevant interviews and they all promised to wait until everyone was together to announce whether successful or not. The atmosphere was charged even before they left for their prospective interviews. Everyone left the apartment and went their separate ways because they weren't sure of the city, they got into taxis. Misty's and Geraldine's appointments where less than a few blocks from each other. Paul, his was the easiest he could walk to his, Carrie and Connie also climbed aboard a taxi. Fate had shone on the two sisters, their future employer were one block from each other, and they could travel together, not always in taxi's though, they had to find out about public transport.

Later that evening everyone gathered around the table and each one told about their interview. They were all relieved that they had acquired their positions, now at least they had money and jobs.

CHAPTER 6

The Pendent

When they were kids, growing up in their family home, had never been easy. Their mother had always been the one that brought love and joy to the girls. Their father, when they had been younger, was full of life but it seemed as though overnight, he changed. He began, as their mother had recalled, seeing the bigger picture; he became power-hungry, wanted to climb up the ladder within their community, he wanted everybody not just to respect him, but FEAR him.

Power seemed to grasp their father; he allowed hunger for power, obsession and cruelty replace where once love lived. The love their mother had for their father started to diminish. He became a tyrant and a brute often shouting at their mother for no reason whatsoever. The girls became scared of their father and rightly, so he was only after one thing: Power!

His power came to surface when one day he came home and told his wife that he had arranged a marriage between Carrie and one of his superiors' sons. Never had Carrie seen her mother so angry. She had called him so many names even now she can't recall them.

*"My daughter will not be used as a porn for your greed and power! **THAT**, I will not allow!"* Rebecca (Carrie mother) cried back.

*"**You have no say in the matter**! The deed is done! Our daughter will be married as soon as she is of age and I intend to make sure that Connie is also married to one of my other generals' sons."* boomed back their father.

Carrie knew she would become of age once she reached 20 years the same as her sister, but her sister still had time. She consulted with her mother... there was no possibility of her marrying someone she didn't love, just because her father was wanting power. Rebecca knew the only chance her child had was to go up into the Earth Surface and mix in with the Earthlings and hide she must. Carrie promised when the time came, she would come for her sister also and help her make a life with herself up on the Surface of Earth. And she promised they would always come to see their mother every chance they had.

Carrie was shown by her Aunty Roberta, the access to be able to escape up to the Surface of Earth. Leaving her mother and sister behind was the hardest thing she would ever have to do, but her Aunty reassured her that she would always keep an eye on Connie and if at any time their father was making the move, she would get word to her somehow. Carrie never knew how her Aunty would do this but seemingly she had her means that were beyond Carrie's imagination.

Carrie wasted no time and had made her way up to the Surface of Earth. She found herself being able to get into a University, as she knew in order to survive, she needed qualifications, and she also needed some sort of employment to fund her studies.

Rebecca always looked forward to her daughter's visits but knew they were both taking a risk as Carl, her husband and father of the girls, would stop at nothing to keep Carrie below, in Inner Earth, if he ever got the chance. So every visit was done in secret only Rebecca and her Aunty Roberta were aware of her visits. But the last time she had come down she noticed that something was wrong. Her mother was very agitated and was constantly looking over her shoulder. She explained to Carrie that her father Carl had found out about her visits and had spies everywhere watching for her next visit. Carrie was aghast her father was that cruel.

Rebecca insisted she go to her Aunty Roberta's home. She would keep her safe until she could get her back up to the Surface of Earth, knowing very well, that her father was frightened of his sister-in-law as he knew, she had more power here than he had and he had to be careful.

So, Rebecca put one of her cloaks over Carrie and told her to cover her face and make her way to her Aunt. She would know what to do; she had more contacts that her Carl and would get her back up and to her life up on the Surface of Earth.

Rebecca was sitting extremely nervous when her husband entered their bedroom. Thankfully, Carrie had left just before he had arrived. *"Where is she woman! I demand to know! I know she is here, somewhere in hiding!"* demanded Carl. *"Who are you talking about? If you're talking about Connie, she is in the garden attending to the flowers."* replied Rebecca.

Carl: *"You know fine well to whom I am referring! Our wayward daughter Carrie, of course. I know she has been here. My spies tell me, so I **demand** to know where she is!"*

Rebecca: *"You must be mistaken Carrie is not here and never been here today."*

Carl:" *"**Liar**! She has been here. Where is she woman, before I beat it out of you!"*

Rebecca: *"I've told you she isn't here! How many times to I have to tell you?"*

Carl became angry and slapped his wife's face hard, sending her reeling. He watched her on the floor squirming to move away from him. Rebecca knew the time had come. Holding her pendant in her hand she pressed the back of it and over in the corner a small green light came on. Tt was a recording device she had installed. She knew one day her husband's temper would lead to something.

Carl began beating his wife, by this time Connie had heard the shouting and came to the door and was stunned to see her father beating her mother. She ran into her bedroom. Surely the beating would stop soon, and she could go to her mother and help her.

After what seemed ages it went all quiet, her father wasn't even shouting anymore she even heard footsteps as he passed her bedroom, and he left the building.

Racing to her mother she was aghast at what she saw. She hardly recognized her mother. She ran over to her. Rebecca was barely alive. When Connie leaned over to her, she knew that her mother was dying; she whispered to Connie to go over to her drawer and take out the pendant that was there, the same as she had on herself. Connie went over and opened the draw; as Rebecca watched her daughter, she reached up and pressed the back of the pendant once again. This would stop the recording.

Connie came back over her mother she knew that her mother wouldn't last much longer. Rebecca told Connie to take her pendant from her neck and give it to Carrie. Those where her last words before she died.

What was she to do? Her sister was gone now so how would she get to her? Then she remembered that her mother once had drawn a map, which she now believed was meant for herself. Connie ran over to her mother's jewellery box lifted the lid and in the hidden compartment was the map. Connie looked once more at her mother and collecting some things she started to go towards the door, but she heard her father approaching with men, what was going to be his explanation now?

Connie ran back into her bedroom and waited. She heard her father groan aloud, then he was shouting.

"Oh, my darling what has ***SHE*** *done to you, what has Carrie done to* ***MY*** *Beloved?"* cried Carl.

For one moment Connie was struck by what was going on, but she recovered quickly enough. She knew she had to move quick. Father would certainly come to her bedroom and ask if she had seen anything. Just how could she say she had heard him beating her mother? Connie had no choice. Connie climbed out of the small window. There was just enough room to get out and run as fast as she could to the entrance to "The Surface".

Carl entered Connie's room and saw that the Connie was absent, going over to window ledge he just caught the glimpse of his daughter running as though running for dear life, he knew instantly she had seen everything. Now what could he do, he had blamed his wayward daughter Carrie, but now Connie was on the run. He knew most certainly she was heading towards the secret entrance that would lead her to the Surface of Earth and to her sister; he had to stop her at all costs!

Thinking on his feet Carl returned to the bedroom and informed two of his most trusted henchmen that his youngest daughter had gone after her sister to the secret entrance to "The Surface". They must capture her. He then went to his facial recognition apparatus and showed one of the men the description of Carrie and he told them that they needed to go up to "The Surface" and search for Carrie and bring her back to face justice.

CHAPTER 7

Science Lab

Present time: Carrie was enjoying her job, in fact they all were, even Connie was getting the taste of fine clothes and would often come back to the apartment and talk none-stop about her day and the ladies that came into the shop.

During the last five years both Carrie and Connie had gotten used to their lives on the Surface of Earth, so much so that they even had a night out with their friends. So much had happened over the time. Geraldine had now moved out and into a new apartment with her new boyfriend Geffrey. He was a nice person and Geraldine seemed to generally dote on him. It was nice to see her friends actually getting on with their lives. After all Geraldine had found happiness. Paul and Misty, well they had fallen out that many times it was hard to remember but always got back together.

Misty had gotten herself a new pad as well and now Paul had decided it was time that both himself and Misty moved on with their lives, but always keeping in contact with Carrie and Connie.

Carrie was enjoying her job, despite it being incredibly challenging and she had shown what she was capable of. Her diplomas had arrived as had everyone else's. She had worked her way up the ladder and now she was in the process of being promoted for her outstanding work, what that meant nobody had told her, she only knew that is was of great importance and she had been chosen.

She was directed to an office on the top floor ... she didn't understand what was expected of her ... she was given a piece of paper to sign. Looking at the paper and reading it she understood this was a declaration of secrecy and she needed to sign it before she was allowed to go to her new job and maybe a new start in life.

Carrie signed the paper and then was given a badge with her name and code number on, the security man told her the number had to be scanned before she could access the lift and it would take her directly to the basement.

Taking the security guards' lead, she scanned her identity badge and the lift opened, and as soon as she entered, it immediately started the descent. She also looked up for no apparent reason and saw the lift had security cameras. It seemed to take ages for the lift to come to a halt and when the doors opened, she found herself facing a large laboratory. But what was even more fascinating was that she was looking at a spacecraft. What in God's name was a spacecraft doing here and how on earth had it gotten here?

Intrigued she started to move forward but a lady, wearing a white lab coat with a high-level security badge, came up next to her and lead her towards a door, opening it with her badge. This lady, whom Carrie later came to know as Dr Georgina Mathews, was the head of the Extra-Terrestrial Project (aka ETP). Now this was something Carrie never in her wildest dreams thought she would see!

"Excuse me Doctor for my curiosity but what is a space-craft doing here and how did it get here?" asked Carrie.

"It was transported through that tunnel over there" Dr Matthews pointing in that direction. "I know what you're going to say: ' How on earth can that happen when we are down here?' simple; that tunnel actually goes up into a steep hill to a secret location." replied Dr Mathews.

Carrie was getting a bit nervous because she recognised this type of spacecraft as being the same type that came from Inner Earth but another sector. Each sector within Inner Earth, housed individual species. The Inner Earth population kept to their own sector never interfering with others. Despite this, they, or we, are all part of in the Inner Earth Nation.

There was a Council of Elders for each species and they would meet to discuss any problems. Carrie knew that her father often attended these but only ever as an observer. Thank goodness he was not in charge here, there would be chaos otherwise.

Carrie was brought back to the present when Dr Mathews addressed her to follow her. Carrie followed the good doctor into a room and what met her eyes, had her nearly in tears. There, in an isolation room laying on a surgical table, was the said individual from that particular spacecraft.

"Is the Alien alive?" asked Carrie, trying not to show her emotion.

"Only just," came the reply. *"We have been trying to communicate with it but without success."* said Dr Mathews

Carrie: *"May I have a go?"*

Dr Matthews: *"By all means but I can assure you that you won't be able to understand his language."*

Carrie walked through the door and looking down at the poor creature she tried asking him in plain English where he had come from (knowing fine well from where).

The creature looked up in hearing Carrie's voice, and started speaking in his own language. Carrie's people had always been telepathic and using her skills of telepathy she spoke to him in his own tongue. He stopped talking and just looking at Carrie he started talking using his own telepathy. He tried to tell her his spacecraft had engine trouble, hence he had to land the craft and he was suddenly surrounded by Earthlings, captured, and brought to this facility. He went on to tell her that he did understand their language but refused to accommodate them. Carrie suggested that he did communicate as she suddenly realized that he was lying here on a laboratory metal bench and it seemed that they were probably going to experiment on him.

Carrie again started to talk to him in the English language and to the utter surprise to Dr Mathews, he responded speaking to her in the Earthling language. Dr Mathews then entered the room and started to converse with the Alien. She was able to discover that his spacecraft had crash landed and that men had surrounded his craft and brought him here. He wanted to know what she was going to do to him.

Carrie was also interested in what was going to happen, but the doctor was still reeling. She beckoned Carrie over and led her to the other side of the room.

"This is marvellous! But they will be using him as an experiment. The other doctors are not like me, they will first use an injection to kill him, and then his organs and such will be removed and examined. I don't like it any more than you do by the look of your face, but my hands are tied. I would like nothing better than to talk and find out all about his world." said Dr Mathews.

Carrie was still talking to the creature telepathically and explaining what was going to happen. She could hear him screaming inside, afraid of what was to happen and asking for her to help.

What was she to do? Could she allow this to happen? She had to think of something, she needed to think!

Dr Mathews led her out of the room and along the corridor to another office, there she sat down and told Carrie to do the same. *"Now tell me how on earth you managed to get him talking? We have been trying for weeks without success!"* Dr Mathews wanted to know.

"I just looked at him and he seemed to read my face and then when I talked to him, he answered, which to be honest, is a shame because now they going to kill him and cut him up. Will they in future years, when more come, will they also be cut up and examined by them?" Carrie wanted to know.

"One begins to wonder ... my whole life had been based on connecting with E.T.s and now I have one here, they are going to kill him before I have the chance to talk and listen to him." said Dr Mathews with some sadness in her voice.

There was a knock on the door and a middle-aged man, plump with beard entered the room. He looked first at Carrie and then at the Doctor in front of him.

"Any news on our patient, have you managed to communicate with it?" asked Dr Francis.

"Not yet." said Dr Mathews all the time looking at Carrie.

"Has our newest assistant tried and had any success?" asked Dr Francis.

"No, she hasn't but we have agreed that tomorrow she can try. Isn't that right, Carrie?" said Dr Mathews with firmness.

"Yes, I would like to try tomorrow", trying to sound excited, *" we just were observing the Alien. Tomorrow our work begins in trying to communicate with the creature,"* said Carrie.

Wondering what Dr Mathews' game was, she waited until Dr Francis had left and then questioned her, asking her why she hadn't told them the truth? Dr Mathews just looked at Carrie and smiled.

"I don't intend that they cut this poor creature up, I intend to try to help free him and get him back to his spacecraft. I think that there is only a small repair needed, and I am sure he will be able to do that all himself. All I need to do now is to keep him alive until I can free him." said Dr Mathews.

"You're going to release him and get him back to his spacecraft? Just how on earth is he going to get it out of here? He would have to go back up that tunnel and I am presuming it is heavily guarded and that the entrance in will be closed..." Carrie said making it sound more like a statement than a question.

"Well, I am hoping that you can help me. That is why I brought you down here, I have a feeling you know more than your letting on, but I also know you are the same as me... you don't want this poor creature harmed." Dr Mathews said.

Carrie: *"For sure I don't, but how are we going to actually get him out of here"* asked Carrie.

Dr Mathews: *"Well here is my plan: At midnight there is only one guard on at the entrance to the tunnel obviously on this side. I plan to get the creature past him and out of here as fast as humanly possible."*

Carrie: *"Excuse me for making a plain observation, but if you look at this Alien, he wouldn't be able to breathe in this atmosphere and secondly, where on earth would you go with him? Have you actually thought this through?"*

Dr Mathews: *"Oh goodness me that hadn't crossed my mind! Here is me just thinking like a human being."*

Carrie: *"Dr Mathews, one thing I do have to say is, if your plan is to work, then you need to think logically, and other than that I have also a sister to think of. So where I go, she goes. I am not leaving her behind to be questioned and mistreated!"*

They sat for a long time and decided they would need to talk to the Alien and find out if there was any way that he would be able to actually help them all escape.

Both the Doctor and Carrie went into the isolation room where the Alien was. They began to talk, he told them his name was Katakana, and that the only possible way for all to get out, would be by getting hold of his device inside of the spacecraft. It was well hidden so that even the Earthlings could never find it.

Carrie in the meantime was explaining her own situation that she herself was from Inner Earth from Sector 1 and that she had escaped from her father with her sister, explaining everything to Katakana. He told her not to worry, his people would protect her if she could get him back. He was in Sector 10. Carrie knew all about that sector and needed to talk with her sister to see if she was willing and brave enough to go back.

Carrie: *"Dr Mathews. I will agree to help you but on one condition that is, that my sister comes with us. She will meet us at the other end of the tunnel, beyond the electric fence."*

Katakana spoke again: *"In my spacecraft there is a* sector *that holds a certain device which I couldn't get to before I was taken. This device would enable us to get away undetected and also allow us to get as far away from here before they found out we were all missing."*

Dr Mathews: *"Where is this device?"*

Katakana: *"I will only give the information to Carrie and nobody else, she is the only one I trust!"*

Dr Mathews left the room and Carrie was given the instructions to where the device was hidden and how to access it. Katakana also instructed Carrie that she must not trust anyone, not even Dr Mathews; there was something about her that he didn't trust.

Carrie also had the same feeling. There was something about this whole affair that didn't ring true, but she would trust her instincts and watch out for herself and this new friend. Dr Mathews asked Carrie if she knew where this device was hidden, she replied that she did, but that she would go and get it herself when the time was right and not before. Dr Mathews seemed a bit annoyed by the look on her face, but Carrie got that feeling of distrust and explained that Katakana gave her instructions not to reveal the hiding place not even to her.

Dr Mathews: *"Okay I understand what you're saying we need to tread carefully though, because we could end up in jail and Katakana on the cutting table."*

Carrie: *"Don't you think it would be better if we both went home and packed our bags, we are going to need clothes, money and food if we are to survive."*

Dr Mathews: *"Oh of course why didn't I think of that? Agreed we will both go home and sort out our things and meet back here this evening. I will arrange it with the guards. I will inform them we are going to be working through the night on something to do with Katakana."*

Carrie: *"Yes and I need to sort this out with my sister as well. I only hope she is up for this and willing. She has just gotten her promotion in her new job and we were supposed to celebrate this evening."*

Dr Mathews: *"Well, why don't you leave now? I will make the excuses and you can have a special lunch with your sister and get things finalized and before you go. I will draw a map of the location of the tunnel and the place to meet your sister after we have gotten out of here."*

Carrie was thrilled she could have lunch with her sister they could make the necessary plans and get things in order. She would tell her sister to ask her boss for a well-deserved two weeks holiday. Carrie is banking on that this would go down well with both the sister and her employer.

CHAPTER 8

Katakana, the Alien

Carrie met her sister for lunch and explained everything that had happened that morning: The Alien and about the escape. She wanted to know if her sister was agreeable to go back into Inner Earth with her, explaining that the Alien came from Sector 10 and had agreed if we help him escape, he will make sure we were safe.

Connie sat for what seemed like ages before a great big smile came on her face. Carrie didn't know what to think; was her sister making fun of her or actually delighted to be going back home to Inner Earth even if it wasn't their own Sector?

Connie: *"Are you really thinking of going back down to our homeland so to speak?"*

Carrie: *"Well….Yes. I am planning to help this alien with the help of Dr Mathews, she will be coming along with us but there is something worrying me also, you know how I get strange feelings about people well I am getting this from Dr Mathews."*

Connie: *"And you want me to get into her mind I suppose."*

Carrie: *"Well, you see, I have tried but something seems to be blocking me or maybe I have lost my touch."*

Connie: *"Has it ever crossed you mind that she is not exactly who she says she is?"*

Carrie: *"What do you mean?"*

Connie: *"Okay. Think about this for a mo. Why were you picked* *for this job? Have you ever considered why there are many in that company older and maybe more experienced than you, but she chose you! Think about this, Carrie."*

Carrie: *"Yeah well, that did actually cross my mind at one point, but I was so glad to be doing something like this that let my defences down."*

Connie: *"Tell you what, I will see my employer and try to get the afternoon off and go back to our apartment and pack everything we will need. I will also let the gang know what is going on. You get yourself back to work."*

"Okay, will do, and if I'm not back by 9 pm make your way to the fence. Here is the map and I will meet you there," said Carrie giving her sister a hug.

Carrie made her way back to work. She entered the lobby and informed the security guard that she was going back down, she need to do some extra work. She entered the lift and made her way back down to go and see the Doctor to explain everything was in hand and that her sister would meet them at the fence once all the personnel had left at 8.30pm. She let her mind go and was brought back to her senses when the lift door opened. She was about to step out when she saw Dr Mathews in deep conversation with Dr Francis. She watched in amazement as they laughed together. What in the world was happening here? She pushed the button again to go back up on top. They hadn't even seen her, what she was to do now?

She came back up to the lobby, the security man looked at her and smiled. Her heart was thudding. What was actually going on? She moved towards another door that led to her old department and saw her friend Edith who was actually the only friend she did have.

"Hello Edith, how have you been and what you been up to?" Carrie asked, trying to appear as normal and calm as possible after what she had just witnessed."

"Gees Carrie you gave me such a fright! What you are doing up here, thought you was now down in the basement where the secret stuff goes on?" Edith said in a questioning manner.

"Can't I pop in to see my only friend here? Listen Edith I need to ask you something; you can tell me yes or you can tell me no, but you know Dr Mathews and Dr Francis. I was wondering if they are friends, like really good friends, if you get my drift," asked Carrie.

Edith looked at Carrie and started to laugh out loud. She just sat shaking her head and still laughing.

"Well you must be the only one around here that doesn't know. But yes! They do know each other and are more than that, they are lovers. Why are you asking anyways, did you walk in on them if so, how embarrassing!" said Edith, still giggling.

"Jaynee! Yes, I did. I was so embarrassed. I didn't know where to look," said Carrie. *" Do you by any chance have a direct line to Dr Mathews I need to let her know I am back and that I needed to ask her something."*

Edith went over to the rolodex and pulled out the telephone number of Dr Mathews and handed Carrie the phone.

The phone seemed to ring for ages before she heard Dr Mathews answer it, "Yes who is there?" asked the Doctor.

"It is me Carrie, I need to discuss something with you for tonight ... if it isn't convenient, I can still come back tonight at the arranged time," said Carrie.

"No, it is fine just come on down," said the Doctor.

Carrie again made her way to the lift passing the security man and again he looked at her, she smiled, explaining she had to go to see her friend Edith. It been important and forgot about it when she had gone down before, security guide seemed satisfied, she entered the lift, and it went down. The lift doors opened, and Dr Mathews came to meet her looking somewhat flustered, but beckoned her straight to her room, but Carrie wanted to see the Alien first and headed towards that room.

Dr Mathews caught up with her and asking her what she was doing, *"I would like to speak to Katakana, if that is alright with you,"* said Carrie. Dr Mathews looked at Carrie then nodded and walked with her to see Katakana, they both entered the room to see Dr Francis leaning over the Alien, he seemed to be talking to him until Carrie saw a vial in his hand.

"No! You can't do that!" shouted Carrie.

"Why can't I?" asked Dr Francis *"He can't talk to us so what use is he? All he can talk is in his own language. Now get out of here and let me get on with it!"* Dr Francis said in a very commandeering voice. Carrie didn't know what possessed her, but she flung herself at Dr Francis and he fell off the Alien landing on the floor. Quickly she ran over to Katakana and removed the vial, standing between Dr Francis and Katakana she looked threatening to say the least. Her martial arts training taught to her by Paul had come in handy.

"What in the Name of God, are you doing?" asked Dr Francis and Dr Mathews together.

"Firstly, I am going to save this Alien! You both seem to have forgotten, he comes from another planet and secondly, you are both going to stay there in complete silence and not one false move! See this vial? One of you are going to get it pushed straight into you and the other, well, I will leave that to Katakana!" Carrie sounded very believable.

She undone Katakana's restraints all the while watching both Doctors, who remained silent. Then Dr Mathews, in despair, broke the silence by pleading with Carrie ... it wasn't her idea but Dr Francis's and to use the vial on him. *"Oh spare me the heroics, you both didn't see me, but I came down earlier and you were both laughing and talking. I went back upstairs pulled a few strings and hey presto you are lovers and not enemies,"* Carrie said very matter of fact.

"***You ungrateful bitch!***" snorted Dr Mathews.

"I may be an ungrateful bitch, but where I come from, we respect other species and do not harm them," disclosed Carrie.

"***I knew it! I knew it!*** *I knew there was something different about her!*" exclaimed Dr Mathews facing Dr Francis now and point at Carrie.

"Oh yes, well done! Very well summarized. I most certainly come from where this Alien comes from, but I come from a Sector different to his. The only reason I am here is because of my father," stated Carrie and facing the Alien she said: *"Katakana please look in that draw and find me some tape to tie them up and gag them."*

"No need," said Katakana he went over to both Doctors and from within his arm he produced a small device he waved it across their faces, and they both fell asleep.

"What in the world did you do to them?" Carrie asked horrified.

"When they wake up, they will not remember anything that has happened here, the only thing that will happen is that both of us and your sister will escape before these two waken," answered Katakana.

Still carrying the device they walked out of the room and down towards the spacecraft, at the bottom of the stairs they came to a halt. A man in a white coat looked up at them shocked to see the Alien walking down the stairs. He went to reach inside his pocket to produce something but before he could, Katakana used his device and the assistant fell down fast asleep.

"Marvellous!" exclaimed Carrie.

"Yes," Katakana calmly replied.

Proceeding to the spacecraft, Katakana walked up the steps and entered it. He came back out smiling with another device in his hands, he looked at Carrie ... they need to get out of here and fast.

"You can't breathe out there," uttered Carrie.

"Yes I can with this little device," said Katakana which suddenly grew much bigger. It appeared to be some sort of helmet, but he just put it over his face and then turned to Carrie and beckoned her to come he was now running towards the tunnel.

"I can't go yet, my sister won't be there at the fence," Carrie said, worried.

"Yes you can, she will be there," Katakana stated. *"Your sister is highly evolved in telepathy; she will have gotten my message that the plans had now changed to a much earlier time."*

Both Carrie and Katakana moved slowly down the tunnel keeping the noise down, they crept along it until they came to the entrance and saw the security man guarding the entrances.... this was awkward ... they didn't have Dr Matthews with them.

Carrie stepped out and made her way towards the security guard making sure Katakana kept in the shadows.

"Miss, you're not allowed down here. Kindly go back, this is a restricted area," ordered the guard.

"I am so sorry, I didn't know. Dr Mathews did mention that this tunnel leads to the outdoors and I just had to come and see, can you tell me how it works I am so curious," Carrie said with such a big smile the guard seemed to relax. Carrie knew this man was too big to handle much less knock him off his feet. What was she to do? Then she remembered what Paul said: You only think you're not strong but believe in yourself and your strength.

Carrie approached the guard who had turned to show her the panel, when she took his legs from beneath him and landed him a karate blow that knocked him out cold. Katakana came out from his hiding place looked at the size of the guard and then at Carrie; she would be some force to reckon with and he reckoned her father was in for a big surprise a noticeably big one; his little girl was now no longer the little girl.

CHAPTER 9

Witness Report

Outside of the perimeter Connie was waiting; she didn't know why she was here at this time, but it was as though someone had telepathically tuned in to her head and told her to come sooner.

Connie watched the open space and waited. She knew the tunnel entrance was not far away, but they would be in open grounds before they got to the fence, she hoped against hope that nothing would go wrong.

Carrie in the meantime was getting the door opened and thanked Dr Mathews for the code, the door opened and they both walked through it but out into open land. Carrie knew that if Dr Mathews had lied, they would have easily been captured so what now?

Katakana, touched her arm and pointed towards the fence where she could see her sister plainly. They both went down on a crawl towards the fence they kept stopping expecting for something to happen, but nothing did, maybe because they were actually early. Maybe that was it.

They reached the fence and both sisters looked at each other from opposite sides of the fence.

"What now Katakana?" asked Carrie

Reaching inside the small bag at his side, which Carrie had failed to notice, she watched him place it near the fence and the electricity in the fence got switched off, he then started to cut the wire, but Carrie couldn't tell with what. Once the gap in the fence was big enough, Katakana beckoned for Connie to step through. Connie stepped through and all three stood there in the opening. 'What was going to happen now?' both Carrie and Connie were thinking. Just then, before either of them had spoken, they were enveloped in a pinkish type of light and they seemed to lift of the ground and into the air. Both girls looked at Katakana, he looked up, they followed him looking up and there they saw a giant spacecraft. 'How on earth had that get here?' thought Carrie.

Time for Q&As would come later but as they ascended into the spacecraft, they thought as though in union 'here we go the next adventure begins.' They were met by some other alien crewmembers. Katakana introduced Carrie and Connie to the Commander, whom Katakana addressed as Commander Caranda, explaining, as they walked to the control room, how Carrie and Connie had helped to rescue him and of their mission to go back with them into Inner Earth, where they will decide the best way to go forward. The Commander listened with great intent as Katakana illustrated the exact way the girls had come to be up on the Surface of Earth. That their father had killed his wife and their mother but had blamed Carrie for it, even though she was only secretly visiting her mother, somehow her father had found out by the many spies he had placed in position around their home watching for her to come. Carrie went onto explain that she had left her mother alive but had that feeling her father was coming, and had gone to her Aunty Roberta, her mother's sister, so that she could escape once again up to the Surface and continue with her life.

Connie then went onto explain the full position how she had witnessed her mother being killed by their father, how she had fled to contact her sister and how she was captured and held captive by some of her father's henchmen. Father's whole intent was to shift the blame from himself onto her sister. He did it with calculated disregard for anyone but protecting himself and discrediting his oldest daughter.

The Commander listened but then he said: *"We have heard of you as many people have been looking for you within all the* sector *s as well as above the surface. I do believe you, but I must warn you that your father is now in a greater position than previously when you left. He is now one of the higher elders and therefore sits on the governing bodies that regulate all the sectors inside Inner Earth and it will be only a miracle if you can justify yourselves."*

Connie looked at her sister and realized that maybe they would never be able to prove her innocence if he is now someone of importance.

"Do you have any kind of proof of what your father did, perhaps a recording or visual proof of your father's guilt to present before the higher authorities?" Asked the Commander.

Both Carrie and Connie looked at each other, shaking their heads in union. They felt deflated. What were they going to do? If they returned to their own sectors, it would be to be trialled and found guilty and that was not a prospect that Carrie and even Connie wanted.

"You say that you have an Aunty who would believe you. Maybe if one of our own people could contact her on your behalf and find out what to do, that would be a start but our people have to be careful when dealing with things as we could also be accused of harbouring a person wanted for murder of their mother." Stated the Commander.

"I understand the risk you would be taking but if you could do this for me then we would be grateful. Please do not put yourselves at risk; if anything else I would just have to go before the authorities and plead not guilty and take my chances." Replied Carrie.

"Please, it is the least we can do for helping one of our own escape before being harmed by a Surface person." answered the Commander. He invited them to come into the Command centre and

looking out Carrie could see that they were now descending into a crater. This was the entrance to their sector, the Commander explained. He walked over to the monitor and began talking to someone below explaining what was happening. He looked at Carrie and Connie and nodded reassuring them that all was fine.

After safely docking the spacecraft the door opened and they were greeted by what looked to be high officials. As they stepped off the craft Katakana approached one of the officials and they exchanged what Carrie termed to be a greeting of importance, she was to learn that this was in fact his father. The same official greeted Carrie and Connie and after a few exchanges between Katakana, the Commander, the official bid them follow him and the others were led to a building and shown a place, where they could freshen up, get changed and rest. Left to their own devices, Carrie and Connie faced each other wondering if this had been the right decision to make but both knew that the time had come to act upon things.

Twenty minutes later Katakana announced his arrival and asked them to follow him to another room, when they entered, they were surprised to see many Aliens seated at a semi-circular table.

"Don't be alarmed, we only want you to explain to us here exactly who you are and your purpose in being here in Inner Earth and although Katakana has explained to his father, we would prefer the full details from yourselves." Said one of the other officials.

"It is hard to explain. I can only tell you the details that I know and then my sister can follow up with further details, if your so wish." Replied Carrie.

"Please that would be most welcome," answered the same official.

"My life has been that of resisting my father and his dominating ways. I have never been afraid of him, but I wanted to decide my own

life and not the one that he proposed, also I wished to experience life on the Surface of Earth. This I did with the blessing of my mother who I would visit secretly and also my Aunty. On one occasion I had that feeling of being watched, and on my last visit to my mother she had warned me of my father's insistence, suspecting I was visiting her, so I left my mother to visit my Aunty before returning to the surface. Under no circumstances did I do any harm to my mother I loved my mother, but she was dominated by my father and always afraid of him." Carrie said with a firm voice but could not hide the sorrow.

"I will now pick up where my sister has left off. On her last visit to see our mother my father came back early. Carrie had already left to visit our Aunt so was nowhere near my mother. I was out in the woods, on my way home, when I heard, what sounded like screams. I followed the screams and then I heard shouting. I recognised the voices. They were coming from inside of home. The voices belonged to our parents. I ran up to the window where all the commotion was. I stared; I was frozen in horror. I sneaked into my room and waited. I was afraid of what I might see, and my father sounded incredibly angry, accusing my mother of hiding the fact of my sister's visits, and that he knew she had been and wanted to know where she had gone to. My mother kept telling him he was wrong that Carrie had not been this time, he shouted that he knew she had been, as he had people watching for her coming. My mother screamed at him that she would never tell where Carrie was, at which point my father hit her so hard, she fell, and her head fell onto a heavy table and she collapsed. My father was panicking, and he left the room and, at which point I went to her and knew that she did not have long; she was weak, and blood was under her head. She told me to take a pendant out of the drawer and this was to be mine. She then told me to take hers from around her neck and that I must give it to Carrie it was of extreme importance at the time I never considered why. I heard my father coming back with men, so I hid again. He was shouting that his daughter Carrie had an argument with my mother and in the act of temper had killed her by pushing her.

I decided to run to my room and lock the door, I could hear my father issuing orders and stayed quiet, when I thought the coast was clear I made for the entrance. Mother had initially told me about how to get up to the Surface of Earth and where my sister could be found in case of an emergency. I made my way by climbing out of my bedroom window, but I guess I must have been seen by some-one and was apprehended, when I got to the place where Carrie found me when she was also taken." Stated Connie.

"This is extremely grave, and I can understand you're having to flee. And I understand you're having to help Katakana to be freed." He paused for a moment, he was having to think this through and then continued: *"We shall do whatever we can to contact your Aunty, but in the meantime, I think that only those in this room should know of your existence here in this* sector. *Does everyone here present agree?"* The elder faced the group. One by one they answered with a resounding **YES!** *" Done! Will you, Commander Caranda escort these brave young women to appropriate quarters where they will have to be kept confined, until we can contact their Aunt and find out exactly what the current position is."*

"Thank you!" Carrie and Connie responded in union.

They were escorted to the quarters and found them to be adequate to their needs. And for their short confinement, they could accept this and knew that it must be done. If their father knew exactly where they were, he would not hesitate in a flash to ask for them back in fact demand it, and these Aliens would have no choice but to do so.

CHAPTER 10

"Earthlings of the Surface never see us"

Carrie sat down to get her thoughts together, she needed to keep her sister safe, because the minute her father got hold of her goodness knows what he would do. Deep in thought, Carrie was going through her mind for the first time: why had this ever happened and most importantly why had her mother insisted that Connie give her a pendant, one that was the same as hers ... was this something to do with her death? She needed to get in contact with her Aunty as soon as possible maybe she would shed some light on it. Still deep in thought Carrie became alert when Katakana entered the room, he looked stressed; what was going on?

Walking over to Carrie he also motioned that Connie joined them.

Katakana: *"I have just found out that one of the other Elders knows your father and thinks that it would be more trouble than it is worth hiding you here and has demanded that you be returned to your own people as this race doesn't need the repercussions of harbouring a murderer."*

Carrie: *"Oh my goodness! What are we to do if we are taken back to our father? There will be no way that I can prove my innocence, he will make sure of that! You don't know our father and I would imagine that over the years he has been afraid of mine/our* (gesturing towards Connie*) return; as he will be safely thinking, all he has to do is capture me and put me on trial without reference to why I am sup-*

posed to have done it."

Katakana: *"Your father has been contacted but I assure you that you will not go anywhere, if you don't want to. And now I think it is best if I take you to a secret place that only myself and the Commander know about. There you will be safe. The Commander is waiting outside to escort us."*

Carrie: *"But won't that make the Elder angry and hold you responsible?"*

Katakana: *"Not if they don't suspect that we have helped you. As far as they will know is that you felt the need to go into hiding ... somewhere in one of the other* sector *s, and on second thought, maybe that is an even better idea. Some Aliens in the other* sector *s, I believe don't like your father, let me check up with the Commander as he knows many of the commanders and leaders of several of the alien* sector *s. He can make enquiries for you, but I tend to think for the time being it would be better to move you now."*

Carrie and Connie once again picked up their belongings and followed Katakana. They left the quarters and following in the wake of the Commander, who never uttered a word, he just walked ahead, and they followed. They seemed to go through many parts until at last they came to a small cavern covered by foliage. It was hidden from prying eyes and nobody would ever think to look for them here while the Commander made the necessary enquires. On entering the cave, they were astounded to find that there was bedding and food already there. Why? Turning to Katakana for an explanation the Commander spoke: *"I anticipated the reaction of one of the Elders, so I collected some items and left them here. When I was sure that the Elder in question was making contact with your father, I knew immediately that you needed to come here and not wait."*

Carrie: *"Thank you, and I do appreciate all that you have done for us, but I don't want you both to be in trouble with your Elders over this."*

Commander: *"Trouble is what we thrive on isn't it Katakana? We revel in making as much trouble for this one Elder who is corrupt and needs to be taken down."*

Katakana: *"We will leave you both here now and get back to our duties. As soon as the necessary enquires have been made and we can get you safely to another* sector, *the better it is for all involved. Many of the other Alien races live in "harmony" as long as each keep to their own* sectors."

Katakana and the Commander left. The cave was warm, and they settled down for that evening. They knew this could possibly take a few days and they needed all the strength for the coming days or even weeks. Carrie decided in the meantime to teach Connie some of the self-defence movements, that she had been learning in martial arts. The next day, Connie and Carrie spent practicing and going through different positions and movements, Connie was a quick learner and picked up a great deal of the movements, which took Carrie aback.

Mealtime came and went, and they settled down for the night. They were exchanging memories of their mother for the first time since her death. Sharing the memories of all the happier times when their father had been a loving and generous father, until the thought of power and money had taken him over and just like that overnight he seemed to change. They sat and held each other in arms, crying when realising that their mother was gone, to never return again. What was to become of them? They needed to fight their father but with what? They didn't have any proof or even evidence unless their Aunt knew of anything ... maybe, just maybe they would be able to prove that it was their father's furious act of temper that had taken the life of their sweet beloved mother.

Morning came and no sign of either the Commander or Katakana. They hoped that nothing had happened to either of them. They had their stories together: Katakana had come to their quarters to find they had gone missing and had contacted the

Commander and they had spent many hours looking for them without fail before reporting them missing.

By afternoon Carrie was starting to get really worried still no sign of their friends – yes, she now classed them as friends. What on earth could be happening, Carrie knew she dare not go out of the cave for fear of been seen, Connie was now pacing the floor and was getting on Carrie's nerves. She told her sister to sit down, there was nothing they could do until evening and if the Commander or Katakana hadn't returned by then they would make their way up to their own sector and hopefully not be recognised and go to their Aunties home.

At late afternoon there was a sound outside of the cave, Carrie told Connie to move back and out of sight, until she made sure that it was either the Commander or Katakana. Entering the cave was Katakana. He looked at Carrie and it looked to her that there was something amiss, So, she went over to him and began asking him what had happened, could they go another sector?

"First things first! You can go to another sector *the Commander has made the arrangements, but I do have some sad news as well. I made the necessary enquires about your father and your Aunty. I am afraid that your Aunty has been held in one of the prisons and has been there since your escape. The reason being given, and this is your father's doing, he accused your Aunty of shielding you and also helping you escape which she has always strongly denied. But your father's word seems to have been taken. All I can say is, maybe we just have to get your Aunty out and away from that* sector *to hopefully be with you, and then just maybe you can all find a way to sort this mess out and prove your innocence."* Said Katakana.

Carrie stood there looking stunned. Connie was crying out loud that Carrie had to go over to her and tell her to be quiet in case someone heard her.

Looking at Katakana, Carrie motioned to him to sit and tell

her exactly how he had found this all out and what of her Uncle, was he also in prison? Katakana began explaining of the necessities to start to make the plans. The Commander assured him that they would be safe in Sector 4 which was not too far from her own Sector.

Whilst they were talking the Commander entered looking very grave indeed: *"Your father has just arrived at our Sector and demanding to see you, but of course you are nowhere to be found and the Elder is getting frustrated. He is trying to find out how you could have escaped, so I suggest that you stay low for another day until I can figure out a way to get you to Sector4 without being seen. By the way, I have just met your father again and he is still the same arrogant man he was all them years ago. He has even said that if he has to go through every Sector in order to find you and bring you to justice, he will. You are now in his domain and will not escape this time!"*

"Katakana has just informed us of our Aunt's position and was about to tell me about our Uncle. I would like to find out how he is, being that he is a gentleman and would never harm a fly. I am sorry" said Carrie, *" that is a Surface Earth people's expression, meaning he could not harm anyone."*

"I am so sorry for your predicament but yes your Uncle, he is at this very moment in the mines and his health is not that good. I have gotten a message to him and he has told me to tell you, he is glad you have come back. He wants you to get both him and your Aunt away from their predicament and has asked me to help them." Answered the Commander.

"Oh, is that possible?" Asked Carrie.

Commander: *"I have some good men .... and yes .... with Katakana's help I think there is a good possibility we can help them but* (and he paused for a moment) *where will they go? That is the main problem they can't stay in Inner Earth.*

Carrie: *"If you can help them escape then I can get them up to the Surface of Earth, my friends there will help them and keep them* *safe."*

Commander: *"Don't you think at this present time once we have secured the release of your Aunt and Uncle that it would be better that you* ***ALL*** *go back to the Surface Earth until you can figure out how to prove your innocence?"*

Katakana: *"So, what Is your plan Commander?"*

Commander: *"I plan to take some of my men tonight, while your father is being entertained by our Elders, and try to get them back here to this cave so that we can then arrange for you all to go to the Surface Earth."*

Connie: *"But how is this possible?"*

Commander: *"Our ships are always going out and monitoring the skies for other aliens trying to penetrate Inner Earth. There are many of us up there, but the Earthlings of the Surface never see us."*

Connie: *"Goodness me!"*

Carrie: *"Do you think you can do this rescue of our Aunt and Uncle? Aunty is very technically minded, and I am sure will be able to survive for the time being up on the Surface of Earth."*

Commander: *"Okay I must leave you all now, come Katakana we have much work to do, it must be planed to the last detail to leave no errors."*

Carrie: *"Thank you both, and I am sure we shall all meet again after all of this."*

Commander: *"I am sure we will."*

Just as they were leaving Carrie pulled Katakana to one side and asked why the Commander was helping them, but he said that would be up to the Commander to tell them.

Leaving the cave Katakana was deep in thought he trusted the Commander and knew if a job were to be done, he would do it. He had lost his own children in a battle in the sky and had always gone out of his way to make sure nothing would happen like that again.

CHAPTER 11

Plotting the Escape

Up in Sector 1 Carrie's Uncle was making sure that things would go smoothly if a rescue was coming. He had learnt many things and had become very bitter, especially towards his brother-in-law. If he ever came face to face with him again ... he didn't know what he was going to do.

His wife was one of the most loving people ... and to be put into a prison through no fault of her own ... her sister dead and she was being accused of helping her niece escape, which was not true, but even if it was, she would never admit to it. Heartbroken on the death of her sister, her mind hadn't been clear when they came to take him and Roberta away. Normally Roberta is a woman who would fight for the truth ... it had all been taken away. Now maybe with the return of her nieces the truth may finally be revealed. He was only allowed one contact a month with his wife and that one was due today. He had been preparing what he was going to say ... that their nieces where here and they would all be reunited with them again. But over the years his wife had changed, gone was the happy go lucky woman he loved ... her smile had gone ... her eyes where dead.

He went to visit his wife in the special place for couples, on seeing her again he wanted to cry with both joy and relieve, for, whatever it was he saw her smile for the first time in years. Something had triggered this off. Going over to greet her which was allowed she whispered they are here my beautiful nieces are here thank the heavens. Armando whispered in her ear that they were going to be rescued she needed to be ready for that evening. Two Aliens from Sector 10 would becoming for her and the others for him.

"Good! I need to feel them in my arms again, I need to see them again." she held back tears of joy.

"My love, we will all be reunited. I have been told your brother-in-law has gone to the Sector they were last seen at, but I have it on good assurance they are in hiding; not to be found." Said Armando.

Armando and his wife talked about what they would do once they had escaped this terrible situation. They knew they would never be safe in Inner Earth they must prepare themselves to go up to the Surface among the Surface Earthlings, and if their nieces could do it then so could they. After their brief meeting was over, both were escorted back to their sectors to begin their entrapment. Always being watched and they knew why. You see, if their nieces found out where they were being held, they would make every attempt to release them. Thankfully, this wasn't theirs to do but friends of theirs; how on earth had they made friends of these Aliens from Sector 10? He didn't know how, but he was eager to find out. Armando was finished his shift and was escorted back to his cell. He sat and pondered over everything he had been told when he first had been contacted ...'... *I can't take this anymore ... I need to get away from here ... it is killing me ... I was never meant for this kind of labour. I am a technician for Gaia's sake!*' He thought to himself.

Later that evening as people returned to their quarters, nine Aliens where creeping around, keeping in the shadows and all armed. Both Katakana and the Commander where leading the assault. Katakana wondered to himself how he had managed to get these men to follow him. But the answer was simple: These are **my** men and trust they **me** as I trust them. Once the situation and the plan was explained to them, they were eager to help. They split into two groups; the Commander leading one section and heading towards where the Uncle was being held (as that was the trickiest one), and the others, led by Katakana, went for the penitentiary, where the Aunty was being held. The plan was, if successful, they would meet up at the entrance that takes them to their own Sector. So, saying each went their own way.

Armando was waiting for him and his good wife to be rescued. Separately, they were both hoping that their rescue would be smooth, and no one killed. This was also the intention of the Commander. For the plan was for him and his men to get in and out there, without being seen.

The Commander approached the area where the Uncle was being held, he looked around ... only one guard? This is unusual ... maybe the other guards are guarding the other prisoners, but he thought, the Uncle was a special case. Sneaking up, the Commander took the guard by surprise. He hadn't even been aware of the Commander's presence. The Commander acted fast, the guard went down, remembering nothing.

Armando was listening and heard the sound of the key in the lock, crouching back into the corner, he waited, the Commander entered, and motioned to him to come forward, telling him to be as quiet as possible and that some of his other men where rescuing his wife. He would meet up with her soon but that they needed to get away now before the guard woke and sounded the alarm.

Armando followed the Commander. He felt jubilant. He was free! He was free! He was overjoyed to be walking away as a free man.

Meanwhile Katakana had approached the place where the Aunt was being held. This was going to be much easier than he had imagined. No guards outside of her cell ... only one guard patrolling the grounds. They watched as the guard went around and took their chance the minute he was out of sight, using special device Katakana opened the door and beckoned Roberta. Out she walked, out of her cell, Katakana then relocked the door and they made haste before the guard came back around.

"Where is my husband?" Whispered Aunty the question.

"We will meet up with him, my Commander is rescuing him as I am rescuing you and so far, no alarms have been sounded. We need to get away before they sound the alarms, as then, the hunt shall begin." Katakana calmly whispered back.

The two rescue groups kept to the shadows as they made towards their rendezvous point. Katakana knew the trickiest part was getting them through to the girls without being seen. They had sent out scouts to go ahead and check the area for any suspicious movements or anything suspect. The scouts were gone a while, but then they returned and reported, that all was quiet ... noticeably quiet .... too quiet for their own liking.

The Commander thought for a moment and then decided to take the two people through the back way to his own quarters, and from there they would wait until the commotion had died down. He was banking on the girls' father to swiftly return to his own sector, once the news of the Aunt's and Uncle's escape reaches him. So the Commander led the two people to his own quarters and made them as comfortable as he could and went in search of the only Elder, he trusted.

Carrie and Connie sitting in the cave suddenly looked at each other, they could feel a great presence. Yes! Their Aunt was safe, she was using her telepathic powers to send them a message that she was safe, but they had to wait to meet up. Carrie and Connie hugged each other tightly and shed tears once again, everything seemed to be working out and hopefully, they can get back up to the surface and hide once again.

Armando and his wife were settling down, they had washed and where eating properly for the first time in years. The Commander walked in during this, smiling he assured them that they would be safe. He also informed them of the plans that had been made before the rescue, with their nieces, and that they all had to go up to the surface; until, that is, they could find a way to prove who the real murderer of her sister was.

Armando nodding in agreement, he looked at his wife and she also nodded, they both knew instantly this was the only logical thing to do. Suddenly they heard a commotion in the corridor. The Commander told them to go into another section of his quarters and to stay quiet. He went over to the table and removed the remains of the meal and then looked around satisfied that nothing showed of anyone being in the quarters and walked out into the corridor. He saw the Elder, the one he didn't like, shouting that there was something up ... that their guest had to go back to his own Sector ... as two prisoners had escaped, and he wanted to know if any of our people were involved.

The Commander approached the Elder and demanded to know what in the name of Gaia he was talking about. He had been enjoying a quiet evening before his next shift out into the atmosphere. The Elder looked at him not sure how far to go but seemingly satisfied he walked away; the Commander didn't like this he needs to get these people away as soon as possible.

Katakana had also heard the commotion and got curious and went to see the Commander, who explained exactly what had happened. Making it quite obvious to them both they needed to get these people out of their sector as soon as possible. When that was done, they could then get back to their own jobs.

The following morning, the Commander rose early. He urged Aunt and Uncle they needed to get ready and quickly; in the meantime Katakana was in the cave telling the girls to make haste, they needed to get away now. Following Katakana, they zigzagged through the many parts of the community until they reached the section where the spacecraft where kept. The Commander was already there, he held up his hand to stop Katakana from coming forward, the Commander needed to make sure it was safe before all of them boarded. Going forward the

Commander approached his spacecraft and opened the doors, he looked around and beckoned the Aunt and Uncle to run forward and climb the steps into the spacecraft, once they were inside he then beckoned for the two girls to run across and up the steps. Still looking around for any signs of activity the Commander was assured nobody had seen anything.

Katakana walked across the space and approached the Commander; he wasn't coming on this journey as it would be suspicious.

CHAPTER 12

The Hologram

Once aboard they were shown to their quarters by one of Commander Caranda's men and told to make themselves comfortable, they would soon be on the Surface of the Earth, at a place designated by Carrie previously, not too near and not too far from where she lived with her friends. Before settling into their rooms, the girls' Aunty went over and hugged them dearly, crying with both relief and amazement how these girls had managed to survive. She needed to have a wash as did her husband; the stress of everything had taken its toll on them, they felt tired and exhausted and a nice warm wash sounded welcoming.

So, while they were waiting for their Aunt and Uncle to get refreshed, Carrie and Connie talked about what they were going to do next. Deep in thought they didn't hear her Aunty approach and looking up, the girls remarked how much better their Aunt and Uncle looked. All they really needed were some descent clothing and a proper shower to spruce up. They all sat together discussing the last few hours and what had happened, Connie began and with how she had witnessed her father kill their mother, and without proof, they would always be on the run. The only thing her mother had insisted on was that she gave Carrie her own pendant and how she had told her to get the other from a drawer.

Clapping her hands their Aunty asked to see both pendants, doing as requested the girls watched in amazement as their Aunty puts the pendants together back to back. She then proceeded to press the centre of Carrie's pendant and a Hologram appeared, they were all taken aback as they began witnessing the murder of their mother, her sister. As they watched the Hologram in horror, the Commander had entered and was also witness to the horrific murder of the girl's mother and how the callous demeaner of a husband and father just walking away with not a care in the world. The Hologram finished and as it did their Aunt Roberta just collapsed and cried. Her husband went over to comfort her, looking up at the girls he just shook his head in disbelief of what he had just witnessed ... that man needs to pay for all the suffering he had brought.

The Commander approached Carrie and asked to see how the pendant worked the Hologram. It started up again, but Carrie shut it off, as the stress it had caused, they did not need to see this again.

"May I suggest this Hologram firstly needs to be protected, but it also needs to be shown. We have a certain device on our craft that enables us to send the Hologram out. May I also suggest, once we have placed you in your safe zone on Surface Earth, Carries knows where this is, you all return to your accommodation. In the meantime, I will do one of two things: firstly, I will make a secret copy of this Hologram and secondly, I will broadcast it into every Sector within Inner Earth. It will go to every sector's High Council where it cannot be erased and also to every person in Inner Earth. The only problem that I can see is getting into Sector 10 as there your father Carl controls everything that goes in and out in communications." Said the Commander.

"Maybe I can help you," replied Roberta.

"How would you do that? Getting into the Communications in Sector 10 will be impossible," replied the Commander.

"When you are ready to send the Hologram, I will do the command sequence to send this directly to one person. It won't even go through the normal Communication Channel, but directly to the High Council Elder, who has known me all my life and has tried to

help me." Responded Roberta.

"Excellent!" exclaimed the Commander.

The Commander asked for the pendant and was given it, he then proceeded out of the door and towards his command centre. He went over to the device he had told Carrie about with the Pendent and pressing the center, as instructed by Carrie, he connected it to his device and the broadcast was being copied. He was standing watching it all over again when one of his men came forward, also stood watching the sequence of events unfold.

"Commander Caranda, we are approaching the destination. Do I have your permission to go and let our passengers know it is time to get their things together?" asked the crew member, whose name was Dankatia.

"Yes, escort our passengers to the transporter room, but ask the Aunt to come here before they depart, she will need to collect the pendant and also send the transmission to someone she trusts in her own Sector." Instructed the Commander.

Dankatia followed the Commander's orders, all the time wondering why his Commander was helping these Inner Earth Humans. He knew of the girl, Carrie, rescuing Katakana and how brave she had been, maybe this was the Commanders way of payback ....

Entering the quarters of the Inner Earth Humans, Dankatia asked them to follow him to the transporter chamber, and as instructed, advised the Aunt she needed to first go to the Command Station, as the Commander wished to give her back the pendant and for her to send that required sequence code, for forwarding of that Hologram to a trusted companion of hers. As they walked towards the transporter chamber, they passed some crew members, who just nodded their heads in acknowledgement. As the approached the transporter chamber Dankatia, called to one of the crew members coming towards him and asked him to escort the Aunt to the Command Station.

Aunt Roberta entered the Command Station, the Commander stepped forward and handed her the pendants and motioned to her to join him at the console. He showed her that, that all was ready to be transmitted and he only needed her to punch in her set of codes to send to the destined person. The Commander looked at the Roberta and realized he would need to turn away, as this code was confidential. Roberta entered the long combination of encrypted codes and then turning towards the Commander, she tapped him on the shoulder, letting him know, it was done. He looked at her and realized she had sent them all to every single Sector.

"Well since you have more or less done my job for me, shall we proceed to the transporter, to join the others, but before you go take this device with you. Should you ever be in any trouble, press this button it will send a beacon to me whether here on my ship or in my quarters." The Commander offered in sincerity.

"Once this broadcast is Live, which will be soon, I know that myself, my husband and the girls will be in even greater danger. My brother-in-law will seek vengeance and his vengeance will be great!" Admitted Roberta with heaviness in heart.

"Do you think their father has any idea where the girls are now, at this present time on Surface Earth? Because I think it will take him quite some time to find you all, considering the size of the country and it's different areas." Stated the Commander quite matter-of-factly.

They both proceeded out of the Command Station and towards the transporter, on arrival Carrie, Connie, and Armando where sitting waiting patiently. Smiling, Roberta hugged her husband and smiled at her nieces and signalled them to join her to the transportation beam, which would take them to the Surface Earth. Watching, as they beamed down, the Commander shook his head slightly ... he knew in his own mind, that this was only the beginning and he hoped that these Inner Earth Humans where prepared for what was coming. He had made discreet enquires about Carrie's father and what he learned he knew that every one of them was in grave danger once this Hologram went viral within Inner Earth.

CHAPTER 13

First visit to Surface Earth

Arriving some 20 miles away from their home, Carrie and Connie fished into their bags to locate their mobile phones, Carrie was the first to find hers. She began dialling and hoped to reach Paul, if Paul didn't answer, then Misty would be next port of call. She knew Misty was at her new apartment, and that Misty was also having problems with her new flatmates. So maybe this could be a way of getting Paul and Misty back together again. The mobile phone rang for what seemed like ages before Paul answered it. He sounded out of breath but seemed glad to hear from her.

"Hi Paul, can you possible come to get me and Carrie plus two other people, my Aunt and Uncle, I know it's an inconvenience for you, but it is Urgent!" pleaded Carrie.

"Sure, give me your location and I will pick you all up. You're going to the apartment I presume, so will phone Misty and see if she will come over as she still has a key to the apartment and to prepare her for your family members." Replied Paul.

Carrie gave him the directions and put the phone down. Smiling, she turned to her Aunt and Uncle to tell them everything would be fine, but deep down she knew this was only the beginning of their problems, as once that Hologram went viral, all hell was going to break loose and she was sure her father would escape before his arrest and his wrath she wasn't looking forward to. Some thirty minutes later Paul arrived, he got out to greet them all. He stressed, he had to get the van back as it was needed to collect supplies. The all climbed into the van and as Paul drove off, Carrie explained roughly a little of what had happened but assured him, he would get the full story that evening when he finished work. Arriving at the apartment they all got out of the van and onto the street. Roberta and Armando looked around, it was nothing like Inner Earth so much traffic ... would they ever get used to it? For the time being, only time would tell, but they had to make do for now and make the most of it if their nieces could climatize then they hopefully could, too. On entering the apartment block the others, led by Connie, went up in the lift to their apartment, while Carrie knocked on the old lady's door; she stood explaining that her Aunt and Uncle had come to visit and are in the process of renting somewhere near and wanted to come to visit them for a few days while they looked around, would the lady mind? The old lady said no she didn't mind but highlighted that the same rules applied for them as they do for her and her friends and smiled and shut her door. Carrie was so relieved, she turned around and walked across the hall to the elevator and pressed the button and waited for the lift to come back down.

As Carrie walked into the apartment, she was greeted by the smell of freshly grounded coffee. Carrie followed the scent into the kitchen, where Misty was busy making something for them to eat. Carrie had a smile on her face and said: *"Hi Misty! I'm so happy to see you again. So much has happened, will get you all up to speed after ... Misty, look at ye, making coffee and sandwiches.... Thank you! I would be lost without your friendship."* Misty turned to face Carrie and returned the smile and before she could answer back, Carrie continued: *" I guess it was a surprise Paul phoning you out of the blue ... I mean since your last meeting with him wasn't that good ... emmm ... he wanted you to move in with him again."*

"No ... it was fine ... just sit yourself down beside your sister, Aunt and Uncle and I will bring the coffee and sandwiches through." Replied Misty, sounding somewhat "dry".

Misty came in from the kitchen, pushing a trolley, laden with coffee and sandwiches in front of her, telling them to help themselves. Carrie grabbed a sandwich and a cup of coffee – oh how she missed her coffee – and looking around, she noticed some bags in the corner. Looking up at Misty she smiled back at her. Carrie now knew her friend had decided to move back in. Roberta and Armando had never tasted Surface food, but it did smell lovely and they were hungry, so they helped themselves to the sandwiches and coffee. Roberta was amazed and the coffee ... she had never tasted anything so lovely and decided she must have another one. The sandwiches she wasn't too sure of, but once she ate one, she found it to be pleasant and looking at her husband, he, too, seemed to be enjoying everything.

"Geraldine doesn't live here anymore. She moved in with her boyfriend but does still have some clothes here for when she visits, so I guess your Aunt and Uncle can occupy her room, but can I make one suggestion? I think they both need new clothes. I don't think Paul's would fit Armando, but I am sure we can give it a try." Said Misty.

Going into Paul's room she returned with a t-shirt, a pair of denim jeans, and a pair of trainers, not his good gear, as he wouldn't be pleased about that, but she was sure these would be fine. Going over to Armando she handed him the gear and told him to go have a shower whilst the women talked and hopefully the clothes would fit. Armando thanked Misty, and followed Connie's pointing of direction for the bathroom. Armando was amazed at it, although different to what he was used to, he relished in the thought of being clean and clothed. He really enjoyed having a shower ... it seemed such a long time ago, since he last had one. While drying himself off, he looked at the reflection in the mirror. '*My goodness!*', he thought ... he had a beard, something he had never been in the habit of growing. He needed to shave ... but hesitated to use any of Paul's shaving gear.

While Armando was in the shower room, the girls looked towards their Aunt Roberta ... pondering what to give her to wear.

Their Aunt had lost some weight all right, but the girls were confident, that somewhere in their wardrobes there had to be something for her to wear. So Carrie went to hers and started to look ... searching through blouses, pants, underwear and even shoes, as she combed through the wardrobe, she put aside what she hoped would fit her Aunty. Coming out of her room Carrie noticed her Uncle Armando and how smart he looked even with the beard, obviously he hadn't wanted to use Paul's shaving gear.

Walking over to her Aunty, Carrie handed her some clothes and told her to go and have a shower, and that once she had they could all have a better conversation, once Paul was home. Roberta headed towards the door her husband had come out of. This was the most refreshing shower she saw the shampoo washed her hair. Whilst getting dressed, Roberta found herself thinking how fortunate she was that her nieces had come to rescue her, but little did they realise the fight hadn't even begun and she feared not only for herself, and her husband but she feared for the safety of her nieces. Entering the sitting room all refreshed Roberta, looked at those seated as they all turned in her direction, her husband stood up and greeted her and kissed her on the cheek saying she looked lovely. Embarrassed, Roberta laughed and told him not to be so soft, he escorted her over to a seat and they all seated back once again. Misty said that both Paul and she had some exciting news to tell Carrie and Connie, but she would wait until Paul came in, leaving Carrie and Connie just wondering what this amazing, exciting news was to be.

Connie: *"Carrie, I think once we have had a goodnight sleep, we need to do some shopping and I mean clothes shopping, Aunt Roberta and Uncle Armando definitely need new clothes."*

Carrie: *"Yes I do agree but we also need to get them some identity papers so that they can live up on the Surface Earth and hopefully get jobs to help themselves to get established, and I am sure we can obtain* *good references for them both."*

Roberta: *"Girls, what exactly are you both talking about? I don't know anything about the types of jobs available. You know I've only worked in communications and your Uncle was a graphic designer."*

Carrie: *"Aunty, there are those kind of jobs here on the Surface Earth that you would be more than qualified for and you may just gain more understanding of what it is to live up on the Surface and as for Uncle Armando, he can easily get a position with his qualifications."*

Both Armando and Roberta realized that not only were these girls serious but were more than capable of living on the Surface of Earth and well as Inner Earth. In fact they realized that these girls were particularly important and would become ambassadors for both Inner and Surface Earth; they just hadn't realized it yet. Only one thing they did know was, that they needed to help the girls with expenses and to also persuade the girls to move once again. They seemed settled here but there was so much research to do on where they would actually be safe and be able to survive this world for the time being.

But that would be a conversation they would have once they got these necessary papers and jobs in the meantime, but these should only become temporary jobs ... it was now up to them now to keep their nieces safe from their father.

CHAPTER 14

Following a Trail

Carrie's father, Carl, had been receiving some Intel ... maybe rumours, about him being imprisoned, about information circulating that could or would destroy HIM ... something to do with a Hologram that had been sent to every Sector with Inner Earth, every Sector except Communications Control ... every Sector .... EXCEPT Communications! It suddenly hit him, like a slap in the face: Carl surmised that it must have gone directly to the High Elder. He was sure that Carrie and her Aunt where behind this but how in Gaia's name had they obtained this evidence, this Hologram everybody is talking about? He thought back to when he had returned to the Home, before his dead wife had been removed, and that he had on one of his searches discovered that his wife's pendant and another one where missing. Those had been meant for the girls. But this Hologram, had there been somebody witnessing and recorded everything, or had she somehow had a device recording his actions and if so, he was in serious trouble. Sitting there and thinking, he knew his only option was to also go up to the Surface Earth and he vowed that he would seek revenge on his daughters and their Aunt and Uncle, they had destroyed him, but he would ultimately destroy them.

Packing some of his belongings into a bag, he went over to a drawer and took out his gun. It was different to the ones on Surface Earth in fact much more powerful. He looked around his home checking, making sure he had packed everything he needed and advanced towards the entrance to Inner Earth. Carl had it all planned out in his head. First port of call would be this University to see the Professor, he was sure that he had details of the whereabouts of his children and he would make sure the Professor would give him all the information he required.

Carl reached the Surface of Earth and made his way to the University. He knew he would need to tread carefully as at this time of day there would be many students around and he didn't want to draw attention to himself. Once he reached the University, he went straight over to the reception area and asked to speak to Professor Richardson, only to be told he wasn't available. The Professor was no longer with them, he had now retired to another country but did come back to his other home in the country. Dam thought Carl, what to do now? He looked around and decided that he needed to do something, he then asked the receptionist if she knew where the other home was.

Looking at him the receptionist thought this man is not a good man, and politely told him that information was privileged information and that she couldn't possibly give out that address.

He supposed that some students just might know where this Professor lived, so he hung around, looking at some of the students, noticing a bunch of them he approached them and began asking if they knew where Professor Richardson lived. Looking at the man one of the boys said that there was a chance he could still be in his home, as he was about to retire to another country and if it was important, they did have his email address but not his home address. Thinking quickly Carl asked if they could give it to him and one boy produced a bit of paper and pen and wrote the email address down. Carl thanked them, which was not his norm, but he needed to keep a low profile he asked if there was a place around that he could use to send this Professor Richardson an email. The boys pointed to a place just in sight, it was they explained, an Internet Café where he could go in and log on to send the email but if he didn't have an email account, he would need to open one. Carl thanked them once more and walked across to the Internet Café. As he stepped into the Café he looked around and noticed a few people on the computers, but one was vacant he asked the man at the desk if he could use that computer. He was told he could and that it would cost him a dime.

'*What in hell was a dime*?' he thought, he tried to explain he was new to the area and didn't have any money until he got some but if he could just use the computer, he would gladly reimburse him. The man laughed and asked, "*do I look like an idiot*?". One of the men at the computer walked over handed the man a dime and told the man it was on him.

As Carl sat at the computer he wondered if all Surface Earthlings where like this, but he would soon find out. Un-noticed at the other end of the room sat Arthur. He was curious, so walked over to the Carl, he could see he was having a problem. So Arthur offered to help him only for the convenience of finding out more about this stranger. While Arthur stood next to Carl, he got a feeling that something was not right about him.

Arthur: "*You are having a problems, mate?*"

Carl: "*Yes, I've never worked one of these things before and I could do with some help that is for sure.*"

Arthur: "*What you are you trying to do?*"

Carl: "*Well I want to send an email, but I guess I am supposed to create a new one.*"

Arthur: "*Okay, to create an account all you need to do it enter you details, name etc and where you are living and what handle you want to use.*"

Carl: "*Can you help me a little?*"

Arthur: "*Sure, let's get you set up first and then you can proceed to send your email.*"

Carl sat, watching the young man creating an account with

all the false information he had provided and once that had been done, Carl asked the young man, how to send an email. Arthur showed him all he had to do was click on "new email", enter the details of the recipient, and then just write his message and send.

Carl followed those instructions, entered the email address and turning to Arthur thanked him for his help and proceeded to write out his email. Carl wrote that he was wanting to contact his daughters and that he wanted to know if he knew where they were. It was a matter of urgency and pressed sent. He waited a few minutes, and a reply came back, asking what the urgency was and yes, he knew roughly where they were but not exactly the address ... only a P.O Box ... he could give him that so he could write to them but that was all he had. Carl replied he was grateful if he could provide him the P.O. Box address, he would write to them and asking them to go meet him. Closing the email account Carl left the Internet Café, crossed the road to a Post Office and went into the Office to inquire about sending a letter to a certain P.O. Box.

As Carl left the Internet Café, Arthur logged into that man's account and reading it he realized this was Carrie and Connie's father. He was here and on the hunt for them and it looked like the Professor had given him the P.O. Box number. It wouldn't take long for the father to find them from that address.

Now alerted, Arthur knew he had to warn Carrie about their father and although he didn't actually know this yet, he was about to play the biggest role in Carrie's life than he even thought possible.

He picked up his mobile and sat at the window. He had watched the father enter the Post Office and now he was leaving and heading towards the Bank. Did he have a bank account or was he going to use fake I.D.? That was not his concern. His main concern was getting in touch with Paul.

Dialling Paul's number, it was taking absolutely ages, it rang and rang then Paul came on the line. *"What's up?"* asked Paul.

Arthur: *"Well the bad news is that Carrie's father is up on the surface and contacted the old Professor, his memory isn't that good, but he has the information of the P.O. Box account and where it is. My gut instincts say he is about to come your way as he has just this minute come out of the bank and heading towards the taxi rank."*

Paul: *"And the good news is?"*

Arthur: *"The good news is I'm going to grab a few things and get on my motorbike and head your way I should get ahead of him. Whether he is going to fly or go by bus or train I don't know. All I do know is I'm on my way Bro!"*

Paul: *"Holy Chamoli! Carrie and Connie brought their Aunt and Uncle up from Inner Earth. In fact rescued them and I think they need new I.D's."*

Arthur: *"Okay, send me details. I will pass on to my mate and get the ball rolling whilst I'm on my way. He can post them to that P.O. Box address. In the meantime go and bring the girls up to speed."*

Holy Cow! he thought more trouble, at least Misty was preparing the new apartment over the Martial Arts and the old lady didn't have a clue where he was working nor Misty, they had kept their profiles low.

CHAPTER 15

New Acquaintances

Paul packed up his gear and headed for home, he was worried not for himself but for the girls. He knew something drastic had to have happened for the father to come up to the surface, to find them. Paul just needed to get home quickly and find out.

Walking into the apartment complex's lobby, he quickly went up in the lift and entered the apartment. He saw that Misty was laughing, it was a joy to see her there again and wondered what there was to laugh about. They all turned around to greet him but on seeing his expression they quickly realised something had happened. Misty got up and walked over to Paul and looking at his eyes, intuitively knew, something serious had happened and the quicker he explained the better.

"What happened?" asked Misty.

"The girls' father has come up to the surface quicker than they thought, he is actually on his way here. He found out the P.O. Box from the ole Professor, can't blame the old man. Your father must have been very persuasive to make him give him the address but thankfully not the apartment address." Said Paul.

"And now it begins," proclaimed Roberta.

"Arthur, as we speak, is packing a few things and heading our way, but I need to take a photo of your Aunt and Uncle and their false names so that he can sort out their new I.Ds before he leaves. He is sure your father flagged down a taxi to bring to either airport or bus station, in either case it will take a bit to get here." Replied Paul.

Taking out his mobile he instructed that Roberta and then Armando stand still whilst he took the necessary photos and the names they wanted to be known as. Roberta said she wished to be known as Bertha if possible and Armando wanted to be called Amos. Again, using his phone, he sent the photos and the details to Arthur. He got a text back saying he was sending it to his other mate and that he was on his way. He had passed the bus terminal had seen the father get on board a bus so that meant gave them at least over four hours to get sorted.

Misty, while looking at Paul said: *"Go on, tell Carrie our good news and just maybe it has come just in time."* He explained that he had been offered an apartment above the Martial Arts studio and had planned to invite Misty back into his life, but when he got back here, looking over and seeing her bags he knew then, she had already decided to come back and was thrilled. Paul continued to explain that the apartment was ready to move into, all they needed to do was pack their things and make sure that nothing was left behind, no trace of them ever having been here. If Carrie's father should gain entry into this apartment, which he doubted but wasn't taking any chances, he should never be able to tell they had ever set foot into this place. Now facing them, Paul addressed them: *" Carrie, Connie, Roberta, Armando, you know best how you can find and trace one another, so make sure, you leave no trail of evidence behind."*

"Oh, thank goodness for that! Can we move everything over right now or is there something we need to do, like inform the landlady we are giving notice?" Connie wanted to know.

"I will go and explain to the old dear," said Carrie.

Carrie left the apartment and went back down the stairs to the ground floor and knocked on the landlady's door.

Landlady: *"Good evening dear."*

Carrie: *"Good evening."*

Landlady: *"What is it my dear, has something happened?"*

Carrie: *"Yes, something important has come up and we have all to leave immediately ... you could say ... it is life or death."*

Landlady: *"Are you all in danger? I did think something was amiss with you all, as I felt the emotions coming from you all for the first time, is there anything I can do to help?"*

Carrie: *"We have agreed to give you an extra month's rent to help you out until you find a new tenant, but we need to be out in the next few hours. I must ask, if a man who is my father, comes calling, you don't know where we have gone. He may come across all nice, but he is not believe me!"*

Landlady: *"Well as far as I know you moved out two months ago with no forwarding address. How is that for you?"*

Carrie bent over and kissed her and handed her the extra month's rent, which she refused, telling her to keep it as she seemed to need it more that she did. Shocked at the generosity of the lady she walked away with a tear in her eye. Going back up to the apartment she had never seen anyone pack up as much so quick. Even Geraldine's stuff was all packed up; she often came back if she fell out with her boyfriend, oh good grief! They needed to contact her also.

Carrie picked up her phone and gave Geraldine a brief outline of what had happened and told her where they would be and that all her stuff had been packed up. Geraldine told Carrie she was staying put where she was and that she would get her boyfriend's brother to come and pick up her stuff from Paul's new place. Putting down the mobile phone and looking around she just couldn't understand how everything had been packed up so quick but knowing her friends and her aunt and uncle it had happened that quick. They put their stuff outside the apartment and then went back in with everyone helping they cleaned the place up, leaving no trace of them being here which was good.

They got into the lift: Paul and Misty with their things first, then Carrie and her Uncle and then her Aunt and Connie. Once they reached the ground floor Paul told them to all wait there he was going back for the van and they could all pile in would be much quicker and hopefully nobody would see them. Outside Paul, ran all the way to his place of work explaining to his boss he needed a loan of the van to move his gear from the apartment over and explaining he had guests who would only be staying for a week if that was okay with him. The boss handed over the keys and watched as Paul went out. He was a mysterious man that Paul, but he was a good worker, and he didn't really mind the new guests as long as it was for a short period.

Paul arrived, they put their belongings into the van and climbed aboard and drove off to Misty and Paul's new apartment. He reached the apartment only to find that his boss was waiting outside and thinking something was wrong, Paul stopped outside of the building. They all piled out with bundles of bags. Paul walked over to his boss, he explained that these were the guests he mentioned earlier and that they would only be here for a week, as they were going to travel to a new abode but needed a place to stay in the interim.

Paul's boss nodded and came over to help them up with the stuff, he was chatting away to Armando, who was telling him that he was looking forward to his new career as a graphic designer.

Paul's boss, Marco: *"Wow, a graphic designer?! Could you have a look at my posters and help me with some of the designs? I will gladly pay you for whatever you do."*

Armando: *"Sure, once I am settled upstairs why don't you come up and show me what you have in mind and then we can go from there."*

The rest stood in amazement. Just what on earth was Armando doing? He had no paperwork and here he was going to do work on a design.

Marco: *"Obviously, this will be cash in hand."*

Armando: *"Thank you."*

They all went up and put their stuff away, as Marco and Armando talked away as though they had known each other for ages, they seemed to have a lot in common, but how? Carrie could only think it was from the time her Uncle had spent in jail with others, that he had developed this way of talking; as once a long time ago, it seemed he hardly ever spoke. Even Roberta was taken aback at how he seemed at ease with Marco.

Once everything was put away and fresh coffee bubbling away Marco bade them farewell and telling Armando he would be back up once he was finished teaching his last class. Walking over to Paul he asked him to follow him down he wanted to talk to him in private.

Marco: *"Okay Paul what's the story here? These people are not who they seem to be and don't give me any crap. I want to know exactly what is going on."*

Paul: *"You need to ask Carrie she is the one that needs to explain everything. As for myself and Misty we are okay but the others again you need to ask them."*

Marco: *"Okay fine, I will do that once this last session is finished. I will come up and I want some answers and that Uncle of theirs, what's his name?"*

"His name is Amos," replied Paul he had to think quickly on that.

Marco left Paul standing on the street and walked into his Martial Arts Studio, Paul went back upstairs to tell everyone what had transpired and what it was that they actually wanted to reveal. Remembering just in time he needed to phone Arthur to give him instructions to where he had moved to.

Paul: *"Hi Arthur, change of plan. We have just moved into a new apartment. You remember me telling you about the Martial Arts place I work at? Well I've moved upstairs with the rest of the gang, so I'm sending you the google map co-ordinates to show you where we are and for goodness sake be careful! Remember? He knows you!"*

Arthur: *"Sure will do Bro, and I'll be with you shortly. Them I.Ds are ready; do you want them posted to that P.O. Box?"*

Paul: *"That was dam quick!"*

Arthur: *"Told my mate it was a rush order but was a shame I couldn't pick them up. They should be on their way in this evenings post unless you want them delivered to your new address, which I personally think is safer."*

"Sugar! Great idea! I'm sending you the postal details now!" Paul said, feeling overwhelmed by this evening's events.

Arthur: *"No problem, will send the details to my mate now and he will post them in this evenings post. Should be with you in a day or two ... I've given your name so as not to alert this father of Carrie's."*

Paul went up into the apartment and all eyes were on him.

Paul: *"Okay ... my boss has sussed something is not right, especially with our guests here, he wants an explanation and I personally think it is better we all come clean. He is not a stupid man ... but a fair one he is."*

Roberta: *"I agree with you Paul."*

Armando: *"We need all the help we can, and I think this man is the one to help us out, he was telling me of all his contacts all over the country and how I could possibly get a job with one of them. Now if this is possible then I owe him that much."*

Paul: *"Arthur is on his way and the documents will be here in a few days but not to the P.O. Box but directly to this apartment."*

Carrie: *"Excellent idea."*

They got busy preparing a meal for them all for that evening, but Connie was deep in thought she knew that her Aunt and Uncle had not enough attire to see them through the next few days they needed to go shopping. But she also knew that neither herself, Carrie or her Aunt or Uncle could leave the apartment with her father on his way.

"Carrie can I talk to you, I think our Aunt and Uncle need new clothes. They can't wear these all the time but none of us can venture out only Misty and Paul." Said Connie

CHAPTER 16

"Tender Hooks"

Paul had noticed the Uncle wearing some of his clothes, so he dug deep into his wardrobe and found two pairs of jeans, a shirt, a jumper, shoes, and underwear (which were new). He went over and handed them to Armando who accepted them gratefully. Paul also went through his toiletries and pulled out a brand-new razor and handed it also to Armando, who could not wait to shave off the beard and moustache. After he finished shaving and throwing a hot flannel onto his face, he took a deep sigh, he felt the pours open up, his skin felt alive and tingly. He looked at his mirror image and gave himself a smiling, self-acknowledging wink and walked back out, to join the others. Looking at her Uncle she was amazed how that little bit of shaving had made him years younger. He looked fabulous! Even Aunty Roberta found her husband was looking more like himself.

They all settled down to a meal and finished it off with a coffee. They had just begun to tidy the dinner table when a knock sounded at the door. They all scrambled to their rooms leaving only Misty and Paul. Paul went over to the door, looked through the spyhole and was relieved to see his boss standing there. He had what looked like a bottle of wine in his hand. Paul opened the door and invited him in, and on hearing it was Marco they all came out of their rooms laughing for being such idiots. Who else would be at the door? Handing Misty the bottle of wine Maroc went over to the settee sat down crossed his arms and waited …

"Marco, on behalf of us all, I want to thank you for letting us stay here for the week and as Paul says, you wish to hear about us and why we are here!" Handing him a glass of wine: *" Well, I personally think you need to take a good glass of wine because what we are about to tell you, is probably beyond your capabilities of a Surface Earthling. Let me first show you something; I am sorry to say it is not good, and then I shall tell you what I know from my point of view and then the girls will tell theirs."* Armando started the conversation.

Armando walked over to the girls he asked for their pendants, then asked Roberta to show Marco the Hologram. Marco sat in silence, stunned and speechless as he witness something beyond his understanding. What was he looking at? How on earth was he watching this ... this, what did they call it? A hologram? ... a 3D-movie like imagery and on top of that, what was he being shown? It was unbelievable, totally surreal, but he was watching a man killing his wife, that much he gathered. Floods of questions popped into Marco's head. Who are this man and woman? What is their story and what has any of this got to do with Paul and Misty? Questions, questions and more questions and he wanted an answer to all of them.

Armando and Roberta told Marcus where they came from and who they were and what had happened to them during the five years the girls were up on Surface Earth. The girls then told their story and what had happened and how they came from Inner Earth and had for the past five years been living among the Earthlings on the Surface.

Marco sat there in silence for so long that the others were getting worried ... would he help or betray them all? Suddenly he burst into laughter and they saw tears in his eyes. "What in the world had just happened", thought Paul.

"I knew it! You are my mother's people! She always had talked about Inner Earth, but I had always thought it was fantasy, but now you have just told me what she has been telling me all these years." exclaimed Marco, still laughing.

Roberta: *"Can I ask who your mother and father are?"*

Marco: *"There is only my mother she left, and her husband from Inner Earth, while she was pregnant with me, as far as I know she was being ill-treated. She had also discovered her husband to be cheating on her, so she left 40 years ago".*

Roberta: *"Can you tell me your mother's name?"*

Marco: *"Yes, her name was Francesca, but she changed it to Francis here on the Surface."*

Roberta: *"Oh my goodness me!"*

Marco: *"Do you know my mother?"*

Roberta: *"I certainly do! She is actually my own Aunt who disappeared up onto Surface Earth forty years ago and as much as they searched, they could never find her. She had simply disappeared."* Tears now in her eyes, as she is remembering those events.

Armando: *"Unbelievable!"*

Marco: *"Yes unbelievable is the word!"*

They talked for ages and Marco told them he would contact his mother and give her the news; he didn't know how she would take it, but he hoped she would want to meet Roberta and the girls. Marco promised them that they could stay as long as they wanted and that he would make sure this Carl would not find them. He would make the necessary plans and the less they knew about them (these plans), the better it would be for them. He would not harm the father, but he would make dam sure he would never find them. Marco was excited ... he really needed to get in contact with his mother. He wondered how she would react; his mother was a gentle soul and if, what Roberta has told him was true, then it would mean that he, too, was an Inner Earth Human. Wow.

Marco knew, the person he called father, was not his real father, but had brought him up as his own, from a baby. Thinking it all over, he came to the conclusion that his stepfather was a Surface Earthling, and so was his half-sister. His half-sister was interested in the Planets and the Stars, this he knew she got from his mother, she was currently studying science and astronomy and was at one of the leading universities for this kind of study, she had been doing this now for six years and was in the process of gaining her Diploma. He knew his mother was planning for the first time to leave her home and attend the ceremony. He decided instead of contacting her by phone, which he had insisted on her having so he could contact her, he decided he would pay her a visit ... a surprise one. Both his mother and stepfather lived in a small farm holding just outside of the city, never being one for the city life they had remained mostly on the farm. Only his stepfather would leave to acquire the necessary supplies.

Now facing Roberta he told her of his intention to visit his mother the following morning, and then turned to ask Paul to open up and run the classes for the day as he was capable and well experienced to do this. Paul and Marco were discussing the classes that were going to be going on the following day. Paul understood the exact exercises and that Marco would be calling up early the following morning before he left, to give him the spare set of keys.

Everyone was deep in conversations, when there was a knock on the front door ... they all looked at each other ... who on earth could that be? Paul moved to the window to look out and saw Arthur's motorcycle and realised his friend had arrived.

Marco: *"Expecting anyone Paul?"*

Paul: *"Yes, my friend Arthur. He will be here to help Carrie and her relatives."*

Marco asked laughing: *"Good Lord! How many more?"*

Paul: *"Only Arthur, he knows what Carrie's father looks like, and he will be the best one to keep a lookout for him. He is quite ex-*

perienced himself in the Martial Arts and has gotten out of many a scrap."

Marco decided to take his leave, he needed to pack some overnight stuff and get sorted out for Paul to take over tomorrow. He had been impressed with Paul right from the beginning and was also thinking of expanding, but with this new experience coming he may needed to wait; he didn't know exactly what the outcome of all of this would be. Going down the stairs Marco opened the door to Arthur and saw his motorcycle sitting on the curb, he liked the look of Arthur who was just about to turn away.

"Arthur, I presume? Paul is upstairs with the rest of them. I am Marcus and I am also Paul's employer, glad to meet you," he said holding out his hand to shake Arthurs.

"Phew I'm glad to meet you. Paul has told me all about the Studio and how you had taken him on which was incredibly good of you," replied Arthur.

"I think it is me that is the lucky one," Marco replied, winking, and got on his way.

Arthur proceeded to go up to the apartment, thanking Marco who was walking away and going into the Martial Arts Studio. The door to the apartment was open and he walked straight in only to find everyone talking, they had noticed him and came to greet him. Paul invited Arthur in and told him to sit down – pointing to the settee - and tell them everything that had happened. Before Arthur did, he went into his bag first and fished out a small folder. *"Okay everyone, for those of you who don't know what Carrie's father looks like ... here have a look"* and pulled out an enlarged picture of him. Carrie and Connie also looked at the photo. They were shocked at how he had changed. Gone was the happy man he had once been when she was younger, and now looking back at them was a mean and angry looking man. Astounded and shocked by the change in her father, Carrie had to sit down while her sister Connie, still looking at the photo, exclaimed that he had become bitter and angry ... and you could see in his eyes ... it was as though he could commit murder! He looked to be on a mission, and they all knew what that mission was.

Paul and Misty had a good look at him, memorizing him, they needed to show Marco this photo just in case he'd come across him. Taking the photo from Arthur, he walked out of the apartment and walked straight to the door of the Martial Arts Studio and entered. Marco was talking to one of the students, so Paul walked over and tapped him on the shoulder, asked if he could have a quick quiet word with him. Marco saw it was important and instructed the student to wait and practice some movements, he would be right back. He and Paul walked over to the office. Once the door of the office was closed Paul produced the photo of Carl, Marco stared for so long at the photo that Paul was getting curious.

"Gees that man just walked past here no more than five minutes ago, I was seeing a client out and saw him walk towards the block of apartments that you and your friend had vacated." Said Marco.

Paul: *"How on earth had he found this place so quickly?"*

Marco: *"Well ... there is a possibility he has followed the trail of the Post Office, they would only normally give the correct address of the person that is registered the P.O. Box, if they can prove they were a relative. It is possible don't you think?"*

Paul: *"Holy smoke, Carrie registered that P.O. Box for us all and had to give a normal address. I need to let the other know!"*

Marco: *"I think for the time being the girls and their relatives need to stay put and also your friend Arthur, he will recognize him immediately. I take it he has never seen either you or Misty?"*

Paul: *"No he hasn't only his two goons who he sent up to find Carrie."*

Paul left the building and walked backed to the apartment's main building door, looking up and down the road he saw no trace of Carl, but that wasn't to say he wasn't in the vicinity.

Going up to the apartment, Paul gave them the information, seemingly it hadn't taken Carl long to find the street they lived in. Paul explained the possibility that since the Professor had given him the P.O. Box number address, he had gone there and told the clerk that he was the father of the person that owned the box, and it was urgent he contacted them.

"Isn't it against the law to divulge the address of that person?" asked Carrie

"Well yes it normally is, but as Marco explained, he must have told them it was urgent, and the clerk may have felt sorry for your father and divulged the correct mailing address." Replied Paul

Carrie thought for a moment and realized that their previous landlady had no idea about where they worked, where they had gone only that they had gone and couldn't give her father anymore details than that. One thing's for sure, they needed to cancel that P.O. Box, and so saying Paul picked up his mobile phone and dialled the post office, he handed over the phone to Carrie telling her to cancel the P.O. Box. After a few minutes, a lady came on the phone and Carrie explained that she wished to cancel her P.O. Box number and that she was travelling so couldn't come into the office to cancel it. She also mentioned that once she reached her new destination, she would go into that Post Office. The lady explained that there was no need for that, and that a simple email would be suffice to cancel the agreement; so gave Carrie the email address of the office and her name so that the cancellation could go ahead. Thankfully, the phone that Paul had was also connected to the internet. As soon as the cancellation form to come through, Carrie filled it out and returned the email, cancelling her P.O. Box. Paul then took out the sim and flushed it away for safety reasons.

Carrie had a feeling her father would be watching the P.O. Box hoping that she would come to collect mail. She also realised that he would soon discover she had cancelled it and would know she was one step ahead of him and that would certainly anger him further.

Arthur, who was watching everything that was going on, was pleased that Paul was doing what he would have probably suggested to him ... he was catching on fast.

"Right I need a postal address to send the necessary IDs for Roberta and Armando," stated Arthur.

"Send them to this address, just put them in Misty's name and they will get here," said Paul

"Okay give me your postal address and I will get onto it now," replied Arthur.

Paul gave the address to the apartment and watched Arthur go onto his mobile and pass on the address, once he came off the phone, Arthur gave the "thumbs up", indicating the I.D's were on their way ... it should only take a few days.

Now Paul needed a new sim, but he had already ventured out and didn't want to try his luck, he went over to Misty and asked if she wouldn't mind getting him a new sim and get some essentials in but not a lot to make it obvious that your shopping for five people.

Misty put on her coat and walked out of the door and headed towards the shop all the time keeping an eye out for Carl. She got to the shops and purchased a few essentials and a new sim for Paul and decided maybe a new one for herself just in case. She left the shop and started to walk towards the apartment her heart nearly missed a beat. Coming towards her was Carl. He seemed to be talking into some device not a mobile phone but some other type, she walked towards him and had to step to one side as he hadn't seen her, which she was thankful for. Misty reached the door to the apartment and looking back where she had passed Carl, he was still talking into the device. She quickly entered and closed the door with a sigh of relief - she had made it without any contact. Phew! Calmly Misty entered the apartment and walked over to Paul, giving him his sim. He looked at her knowing something was amiss and told her to tell him, the others were also listening.

Misty took a deep breath and just blurted it out: "Okay. On my way back from the shops, Carl was walking towards me ... but he didn't notice me ... he was too busy talking into some sort of device nothing I have ever seen before."

Roberta walked over to the settee and sat down deep in thought, had Carl been in contact with someone here on the Surface Earth? She then remembered Carrie and Connie telling them about the father's henchmen. Was it possible they were still here on Surface Earth? Surely, they would have heard about his crime, or had they? *"Listen everyone, my assumption is that Carl is in contact with the henchmen, the ones he sent up to look for Carrie and Connie. If that is the case, then they have no idea about his crime he would have kept them totally in the dark. Now, how loyal they are to him is another thing, but if they are coming here then it is in all possibility they will begin searching around here!"*

Misty: *"Bang goes our apartment and your job Paul."*

Roberta: *"And why is that?"*

Misty: *"Well those so-called henchmen, if they are the same ones from under the scrap yard, they would know myself and Paul and could recognize us!"*

Paul: *"Not in a hell's chance am I running!"*

Misty: *"I agree with you, me neither!"*

Paul: *"We need to make some sort of plans, but I feel that Marco is doing something to help us, so let us wait until he returns from seeing his mother and just stay put. He did say he was gone for only a day* *or two, and Misty is quite handy. I will also be going into the Martial Arts Studio and if those men do come in, I am sure, that all the students and myself and Misty can manage to sort them out."*

They all decided to retire early for the night and made their way to their rooms. Arthur would be sleeping on the couch, unfortunately there weren't enough bedrooms.

The following morning they all had breakfast and Paul was waiting for Marco to make an appearance to give him the keys for the Studio, and then he would be off, he planned to travel in his van, but Paul thought that would be heavy on the juice so had persuaded Arthur to lend him his motorcycle. There was a knock on the door as they were clearing up their breakfast dishes, Paul went to answer the door, Marco walked in and proceeded to hand Paul the keys to the Studio. Paul began talking to Marco explaining that Arthur would lend him his motorcycle that is if Marco could actually ride one. Marco laughed out aloud, he told Paul he used to ride them all the time until he got his Studio. Now the van was the most convenient form of transporting stuff. Marco walked over to Arthur and thanked him, he had already thought to himself that that would have been the ideal way to get to his mother's faster, plus the fact that the motorcycle had New Jersey number plates, made it look suspicious.

Arthur hadn't even given that a thought and gladly handed him the keys to his motorcycle. Marco said on the return, he would park the motorcycle out of view in the garage at the back of the Studio.

Marco left, but not without having given instructions to Paul: any sign of trouble to contact him. Paul agreed and handed Marco his new phone number. Bidding everyone farewell, Marco walked over to the bike and put his bag inside the helmet box on the back of the motorcycle. He picked up the helmet and was about to put it on, when he seen two strange men walking towards him, he turned the ignition and kick-started the motorcycle and sped off, looking into the side mirror, he noticed that the men were watching him. Around the corner Marco pulled in and phoned Paul to let him know the two henchmen were just outside and not to open up the Studio until he came back! It was too dangerous. He would arrange for the necessary cancellations to the students himself.

CHAPTER 17

Family Reunion

Paul looked out of the window after the phone call from Marco and saw the very two men that he had encountered in the tunnel. Ssssschugar! Just how on earth had they get here? Had they already been in the area and searching or had they arrived when Carl had?

Misty: " Paul, who was that?"

Paul: "That was Marco; apparently the two henchmen have arrived and are looking for you all, and it seems that we have to stay put until Marco returns. The fact that he has the motorcycle he said, he would be faster in getting to his mother and back."

Misty: "Paul, we can't run, we just can't, but I agree with Marco. We wait until he returns and see what's what."

So for the next few hours they lay low and talked and talked, Paul and Misty wanted to know all about Inner Earth and now it seemed so did Arthur. Roberta was the first to speak telling them how beautiful it was in their own Sector, explaining that there are 10 different Sectors, but they all lived peacefully together. She began describing the crystals hanging down from the walls and ceilings, and how there was a beautiful lake, and in the center was the grand crystal that gave out the most beautiful energy to everyone.

Armando carried on to described how on the lake there were seashell type boats and when you stepped onto them, they carried you through and onto a river that would then lead you to a beautiful pasture. You could see the cities, they were elevated; the gravity made them this way.

Connie went on to say that when you went up into the cities it was nothing like here on Surface Earth. You enter the different sections of the city, through "gateways" that was not doors, but just a plasma type of separation. The thing they loved most about their home was, that the travelling was so different to here, you levitated to move from A to B; that was the form of transport.

Carrie, while listening to them all giving descriptions, started to really feel homesick for Inner Earth. She had lived on the Surface of Earth just because of her father but she had always planned to return, once she got old enough to face her father. The sound of Inner Earth to the Surface Earthlings sounded amazing, but they knew that they would never get to see it, or so they thought; things were about to get even madder.

Paul's phone rang it was Marco, he sounded excited he was babbling on so fast that Paul couldn't understand a word he was saying, he had to asked him to slow down and repeat what he was saying. Paul decided the others needed to hear also and so put his phone on loudspeaker.

Marco: *"My mother is so ecstatic! I've never seen her this excited in many a long time ... she is wanting to meet her long-lost family ... she says she never thought the day would come and wants you all to come to see her."*

Roberta: *"That's fantastic!"*

Carrie: *"How are we going to get to meet your mother?"*

Marco: *"Easy enough! Paul, you know how to get to the van via the back entrance to the apartment without going out to the front, well I suggest you do that. You will find the van key on the key ring you have in your possession."*

Paul: *"You're going to have to give me the exact coordinates to your mother's ... I can get the directions from Google Map."*

Marco: *"Sure will text you the address, mind you, if them men are still around, I would probably leave it until this evening that way it's too dark for them to see who is driving."*

Carrie: *"Knowing my father, he will have the face recognition gadget with him since he knows we have friends he will be watching out."*

Roberta: *"Not a problem."*

Marco was still on the line and he heard Roberta describe how they could avoid the face recognition device. He was amazed.

Paul: *"Okay Marco, we will be there as soon as possible ... we will ring you once we are near to where you are."*

Everyone started to pack up their belongings, including Paul and Misty as they didn't know how long they would be away they had to look on it as a holiday. As it got dark, they all sneaked out of the apartment, down the stairs and down the passageway to the back of the apartments, opening the door they looked out to see if the coast was clear. Paul suggested they all wait beside the back door he would go into the garage and get the van. It took Paul a few minutes to start up the van and drive out of the garage, then stopped and got out of the van and locked the garage up, got back into the van and drove to the back door. Everyone scrambled into the back of the van, there were no windows. They sat on the floor thankfully they had brought some bedding to soften the floor of the van. Misty climbed into the front and they drove out of the alley, looking around they couldn't see a living soul and went along the road and still watching ... they saw nothing.

They got onto the State Highway and headed towards Marco's family home; confident they hadn't been seen.

CHAPTER 18

Twist of Faith

Carl had been hiding and had seen the van leave he wondered if it was possible that his daughters and their Aunt and Uncle where in that van. He had taking notice of that young woman, who had passed him when he was talking to his two henchmen, something about her she seemed nervous when she had seen him. He had given them her description and they had informed him that she was the one that had attacked one of his men. Carl had turned around, but the woman had disappeared. He was frustrated but gathered that just maybe they would be somewhere still in the vicinity he just had to wait until his men got here, they weren't far away they had also been doing some research had found out where Connie had been working and now was supposedly on holiday. Deep down, he knew that it had been them who had broadcasted that Hologram, damaging his reputation. He somehow had to figure out just how they managed to do this. But he was sure once he apprehended them, he would discover that possibly the Aunt was behind it. He had taken note of the van's license number plate and he had the necessary equipment to track them, he would use every means possible to get his revenge on those two girls, his daughters, who in one fraction of a push of a button had destroyed his career.

Arthur in the meantime had a strong feeling, that just maybe they had been seen. They needed to get off the road somewhere and leave the van. They pulled into a parking lot and walked over to a roadside café, Paul then phoned Marco and explained that there is a strong possibility they had been seen leaving, and they didn't want to lead Carl and the henchmen right to his mother's home.

"Don't worry about that, we have everything prepared. I told you they wouldn't get within distance of them girls and their Aunt and Uncle; there is a big surprise for them all when they get here ... just to use the van." Replied Marco.

"Okay fine," said Paul.

They all got back into the van now puzzled by what Marco had said. What was this big surprise? He sounded excited. Arriving some two hours later at the farm, they were greeted by Marco, his mother and father, his sister was also there, but there were also many others what was going on, thought Paul.
They were all lead into the front room. They looked around ... what was going on thought Arthur, Paul, and Misty. Francesca went over to Roberta and they hugged and cried, she was then introduced to her two nieces Carrie and Connie. With all the introductions done, Marco explained that the others present here, were in fact, which he had only discovered, all from Inner Earth.

Carrie: *"How?"*

Francesca: *"Before Marco was even born, I knew about some of the Inner Earth people who had come up to the Surface of Earth, leaving everything behind. They were disillusioned with the way the Elders were controlling their lives. They wanted the freedom to be able to choose for themselves. They found the entrance and stepped through it and in doing so, helped me settle here."*

Marco: *"My father, I have found out, followed her up and he is not my step-father but my actual father. They tried to hide from his own father, he made it up just after I was born, and he had loved my mother and wanted to be with her so he sacrificed everything he knew to be here and now I can understand my sisters interests. Mine are different. I felt the need for doing the Martial Arts but have since* *discovered my father is also a bit of a fighter himself, he was something like a soldier in Inner Earth."*

Still reeling from everything Carrie looked over to her friends only to discover they were huddled into a corner, not sure of themselves for the first time since she had met them. Going over she led them over to meet the rest of the Inner Earth Humans and began explaining their own roles in protecting herself, sister, Aunt and Uncle. They all suddenly became enthusiastic and wanted to know more of their role in helping their fellow Inner Earth people. A bit embarrassed, Paul related everything, and they seemed excited to the fact that Surface Humans felt the need to protect Inner Earth Humans. But the main question now what were they all going to do? They had a feeling that Carl would be soon on their heels, he was a devious one and if he did have weapons, they would all be helpless against him as the weapons from Inner Earth were far more advanced than the surface human ones. There would be much to discuss so Francesca suggested to all the other families to go back to their homes and come back in the morning, during that time she would discuss with her husband and extended family what the best route was to take. The others left and promised to return the next morning; some of them said they needed to talk it over with their own families, as some of them had children whom didn't know that their parents were from Inner Earth and they had to break it to them gently.

Francesca led her family into her home and suggested the weary travellers get refreshed and Marco would hide the van in the big barn out of sight. As suggested, Marco went over to the van and drove it into the barn, coming out he came face to face with Paul.

Paul: *"What do you really think is going to happen, Misty, Arthur and myself would we be in danger or should we just make out we know nothing and go back to our normal lives, well as much as we can?"*

Marco: *"Firstly Paul, we need to talk to all the others, my mother and Carrie's Aunt Roberta may come up with the answers ... at this present time I am as much in the dark as you are, but one thing I do know is that I am going to go into Inner Earth, if my parents decide to go there, it is after all my actual home."*

Paul: *"I can understand your curiosity of wanting to know where you come from, but can I ask one question? What will happen to your business while you are away?"*

Marco: *"To be honest with you I have no idea. I need to sleep on it all and will give you my answers tomorrow once I know myself."*

Paul: *"Sure, I was just wondering you have built up a fantastic business it would be just a shame to let it all go downhill. I can also understand you are wanting to see your own homeland so to speak, but you have to also think of your life up here."*

Marco: *"What kind of life have I actually had, I've worked my socks off to make this business work, sometimes I have slow times and some are good, but I never seem to have enough money to do other things ... it's a never ending circle."*

Paul followed Marco to the house, thinking: '*... gees I just may be out of a job if Marco decides to go to Inner Earth ... or ... maybe I can suggest that I can run the business until he decided what he wants to do. Would this be a logical thing?*' Paul was still thinking to himself, but he needed to wait until the following morning to see what was happening, certainly it would be an adventure for him and the others to go into Inner Earth, but Paul couldn't see that ever happening, but stranger things happen. AS they entered Marco's parent's home, they could see that makeshift beds were being made up in the living room, and Francesca was busy organising the sleeping arrangements and everyone seemed to be settling down for the night. Marco went into his own room to find makeshift beds there and it looked like Arthur and Paul would be sharing his room. They all settled down and went to sleep, but Carrie was still awake, wondering where the devil her father was with his henchmen. She hoped against hope that they would have time to escape his clutches, she feared for herself and her family and friends.

Carl was heading towards the home of Marcus's parents. He sensed they were expecting him and knew that they most likely would be preparing for him, so he decided to lay low and wait till morning, when he could face them head on. He was confident, he got them now and there was no way, they could escape him now. No way!
What he didn't know is that he was getting into more trouble than even he thought was ever possible.

Morning came, Carrie was up before anyone and decided to make herself a useful by providing coffee for everyone. She went into the kitchen and prepared the percolator and sat and waited. Coffee-Magic ... one by one everyone slowly woke up and she wondered if it was the smell of the coffee. Smiling to herself for the first time in the last few days, she began to lay the breakfast table, some would have to make do with the coffee table or the kitchen bench but she still went on, preparing toast and marmalade, this she was getting used to herself.

Francesca walked into the kitchen, smiling at the pile of toast starting to build up, walked to the fridge and produced eggs and started making scrambled eggs. They would all need a hearty breakfast for what today brought. Once the breakfast was done, dishes all washed up, they all ventured outside and waited for the others to turn up. Carrie suddenly sensed something was off. She looked towards the treeline and could just make out a car, and three men, one was using some sort of telescopic lens homing in on them. Grabbing at her Aunt Roberta she whispered into her ear that she thought maybe those people could be her father and two henchmen. They hadn't moved. They just seemed to be watching. Roberta called for everyone to get inside the house and quickly.

"What in the world is the matter?" asked Marco

"Carrie's father is here with his henchmen; we need to stay inside until the other show up. They will then see we are a force to be reckoned with." replied Roberta.

"Oh goodness me!" Francesca exclaimed.

Carl continued to watch the house and was astounded to see that there were more people than he had expected. He needed to use his wits and was thinking that he has to find a way to separate the girls from the rest of them. As though thinking on his feet, Carl got up and told his men to stay put he was going to go up to the house, he had to try to reason with his daughters, he knew it was possibly too late, but Carl had something other in mind. He would act the loving father until he got them in his grip and then they would know his wrath! Well at least that is what he thought but getting it done was another thing.

Approaching the house Carl stopped outside of the front door and waited to see if anyone would come out, he didn't have to wait long, Marco's father stepped out and asked him what his business was and more to the fact what was he doing on his property. Carl felt a certain familiarity about this man, but couldn't place him right now, he would need to rack his brains, but that could wait. Right now he wanted to get straight to the point and conveyed he wanted to bring his daughters back to Inner Earth, he missed them and wanted them safely back in his arms.

It was then that Carl saw Carrie come out of the house, he looked at this woman in front of him. He could tell she was strong willed, a bit like him in that way, and just staring at him with hate and loathing.

Carl: *"Carrie my dear, I've come to take you and your sister back home. I know we have had our bad dealings in the past, but this is in the past ... all I want to do now is move forward and become a family again, pleeeease ... give me a second chance."*

Carrie: *"**Second chance**! You have to be kidding me, father, what second chance did you give our dear mother or in fact my aunt and uncle? You had them imprisoned and you stand here grovelling ... you are a person who needs to be pitied! My answer to you is **NO**. I suggest you take yourself and your two waiting henchmen and get the hell off this property and out of our lives for good. **You** are a schemer, a murderer and yes ... I say this ... the **murderer** who killed his poor defenceless wife ... **AND** you left her to die alone ... and then you have the audacity to instead of taking the blame yourself, the yellow belly that you are ... you put the blame on your own daughter. I guess your two companions don't know you are on the run yourself, wanted in Inner Earth by our people. Go back and never bother us again!"*

Carl: *"How **dare you** talk to me like that! **I am** your father and as such you should show me some respect!"*

Carl suddenly sprang forward grabbing Carrie, trying to force her into his car. He wasn't going to have a slip of a girl talk to him like that, especially not his own daughter ... he was going to show her.

Before he could even get to his car, Marco came running out of the home and he sprang at Carl, taking him by surprise. He lashed out using every martial arts moves he could muster and made him finally let go of Carrie. Facing both Marco and his father, Carl stared at them with so much hatred, it was unbelievable that just seconds ago he seemed to be the most humbled person. They were standing looking at each other when there was a sound of vehicles coming towards them, it was the other people that had been here last night but now seemed more of them. Carl looked in amazement. Just what the hell was going on, he signalled on his men to come forward, as they had weapons if he had to take his daughters by force then so be it.
Carl's men watched as vehicle after vehicle arrived at the house, they knew Carl wanted them to come with the weapons, he had in his mind to take his daughters by force, but they weren't

brave enough to take on so many people.

They removed the weapons from the car and hid them in the bushes, then proceeded towards the house, they knew Carl would be angry with them, but they also knew, they were no force against all of these people and even wondered where on earth they had all come from.

Every vehicle came to a halt outside the house and people started pouring out from their cars. People with children and even a couple of elderly people, still watching, Carl wondered why all these people had suddenly descended on this house of all places. Still watching, Carl saw his own men approaching in the vehicle they had hired, now the game was up. The types of weapons he had, they wouldn't be a match for these people. Carl waited patiently until his men reached him and going over to them, he told them to open the boot of the car which they did, but to his surprise there where not weapons.

"Where the hell are the weapons?" asked Carl.

"Sir, with all these people ... we felt it wouldn't be logical to use the weapons on them ... it would cause a massacre and the Surface Earthlings would probably want to investigate." said the tallest of the men.

"When I give orders, I expect them to be carried out to the fullest!" bellowed Carl.

"With due respect Sir, there is something not quite right about this whole situation and until we know the full facts, we will not use those weapons. We have them hidden." countered the tallest of the men again.

Marco strolled over to Carl and his men and very calmly told them, gesturing with his hands, that these people were Inner Earth people and had come together to protect their own.

Carl's men looked around in astonishment, something was

going on and they wanted to know exactly what that was. The tallest of them turned to face Carrie, and asked her what exactly was going on, Connie came out from the house and standing beside Carrie, she took off her pendant and handed it to Carrie who in turn took of hers and doing as her Aunt had done, placing them back to back, pressed the middle of hers and the Hologram appeared. Everyone watched in amazement and speechless, at this recording of Carl killing his wife and more to the fact blaming his eldest daughter. Once the hologram finished, Carrie returned Connie's pendant to her and proceeded to put hers around her neck.

Still stunned, Carl's men stepped away from him and looking at him in shock. This man who had once been their leader, was a killer, a wife murderer. One went to the car and came back with restraints and put them over Carl's wrists, he would be taken back to Inner Earth, and stated that Carrie, her sister and Aunt and Uncle must return with them.

CHAPTER 19

Women's Power

Carrie looked around and many where shaking their heads, many didn't trust these men and had all agreed to go back with Carrie and that is why they had all come. Carrie informed Carl's men that everyone was going back, under the one condition that Marco and his father would also take charge of her father, as they could not to be trusted and this all could just be a trick.

They argued it was their duty to take them back with their father, but Roberta then raised her voice at them; they either do what everyone wanted, or they could go back on their own but without Carl. Both men, believing they still had the upper hand, produced weapons from inside their coats pointing them at Carrie and Connie. They seemed intent on taking the girls.

However, there suddenly was a turning point: The people around also produced weapons, but not Surface Earth weapons, these were the weapons they had brought with them from Inner Earth. The two men put down their weapons and agreed to doing what they demanded and, yes, they would also accompany them down into Inner Earth.

Marco went over to the two men and cuffed their hands also and then using a length of chain he chained them together, marched them over to the barn where he again using a chain, secured them to a thick post. Leaving the prisoners there, firmly tied up he returned to join the others. Each one was voicing their own opinions, the children seemingly excited about the prospect of going into Inner Earth, had decided to accompany their parents after all, they were both Surface and Inner Earth Humans in one sense.

Paul walked over to Marco and stating now that Carl was captured it should be safe for himself, Misty, and Arthur to go back to their own lives.

Marco: *"That is absolutely true, but did you know, that in fact Arthur wants to go into Inner Earth as does Misty, they seemed to want an adventure of some sorts, but you can make up your own mind. The business can be put on hold if necessary, until the time of the trial, but one thing I do know for certain and that is that my life will be forever changed."*

Paul: *"Misty said that? Unbelievable! She never mentioned it once to me this morning, I need to have a talk with her before I make my own decision."*

Marco: *"That is between you and Misty but don't take too long. Preparations are beginning to go back ... we have just received the co-ordination from Carrie's friend, the Commander. His spacecraft will come here, and we shall all board it. He has also said he will lead us all to the Sector 1, where we all come from. So I suggest making a quick decision as the Commander is on his way."*

That was all a bit much to take in ... a spaceship was coming for them ... and Misty agreed to go with them? Paul walked over to were Misty was and was talking to her. He wanted to know why she had decided to go into Inner Earth. Surely it wasn't for adventure but what other motive did she actually have, he needed answers.

Paul: *"So, Misty, I hear from Marco that you're going with every-one else to Inner Earth, can you tell me why?"*

Misty: *"Look Paul, the way I see it, we have been on an amazing, if not sometimes dangerous journey with Carrie and Connie. I have always wondered what life is like there. You see, Carrie and I have been discussing Inner Earth, more or less since the word "get-go". I* *am intrigued ... my hunger, my lust to learn more and find out, if all of what Carrie told me was true, I'm taking this opportunity to find out for myself."*

Paul: *"Okay and yes I can see the logic of wanting to go down there, but have you any ideas about why Arthur wants to go there also? I know he has no family to speak of, so I gather it is an adventure for him, but you have family. Well sort of a family ... when they actually speak to you."*

Misty: *"Paul, I am going whether you want to or not. It's not as though it's going to be forever, is it? We will be there to testify about Carl and all that and then we shall spend a bit of time looking around before we come back to the surface, where is your adventurous streak that you're always telling me about?"*

Paul: *"I get the message loud and clear Misty ... umm ... maybe you are right. We should at least see what Inner Earth looks like and being the first ever Surface Humans to actually visit there."*

Holding hands both Paul and Misty told Marco they would both be going to Inner Earth with him.

"Wow that is excellent news!" exclaimed Marco, *"give me a few minutes while I phone one of the other instructors to let him know that you and I both won't be back for a few days. We are going to be doing some important business."*

Smiling at Paul he went away to make his phone call, he was thrilled that Paul would be coming with him. He needed a friendly face; he didn't actually know where this was all leading to but - and that was a big BUT - if he did decide to stay in Inner Earth, he would have to see about selling the business. Marco had thought this over through the night, he was half sure that he would probably stay in Inner Earth but always come back on to the Surface of Earth, so maybe he could still run the business and have a manager run it ... he hadn't actually decided what he was doing, but whatever that was he would make sure that Paul was in the loop so to speak. Right now, he wasn't going to start thinking about the possibility. A lot could and can happen between now and then ...

Everyone was standing and talking when Carrie told them that the Commander was now above them out of sight and that a beam would come down to transport them onto the ship. They would go in stages of 5 at one time. So, they needed to which of them was going in which group of five and to make it quickly as she saw the first beam come down with the Commander and five armed men. The Commander explained that his men would take Carl and his two henchmen into custody now and transport them on the ship and place them in confinement, he would stay on the Surface until the last of the people had boarded.

Carl and his henchmen were escorted out of the barn and beamed up. No sooner was that done the beam came back down for the start of the evacuation, starting with the Inner Earth People.

Going over to Marco, the Commander asked why the Surface Earthlings were also coming to Inner Earth and wanted to know who they were. Marco explained that these were the friends of Carrie and Connie who had been present when the father had tried to kidnap them and would be standing as witnesses at Carl's hearing.

Thanking Marco he went over to the Surface Earthlings, who seemed a bit wary of him until he spoke about his helping Carrie and Connie also and that they had nothing to fear from his own people. They were in debt to Carrie and would always help anyone associated with her.

Everybody, bar Connie, Paul, Misty, Arthur, and the Commander had been beamed up onto the ship. They now walked into the beam and were instantly transported up onto the ship. They found themselves having arrived in the docking area and were amazed at how quickly everyone had been escorted to their various places. Most were in the dining area of the ship, and those with small children were placed into quarters. The ship's crew members had given up their quarters, to offer rooms for the Inner Earth and Surface People.

The Commander escorted Carrie, Paul, Misty, and Arthur onto the command deck to show them the view of the Surface Earth before they descended into the porthole that would take the ship deep into Inner Earth. Paul especially, was amazed, he could not believe, that he was inside a spacecraft, looking down onto the Surface of Earth, nobody would ever believe him. Arthur was bubbling with excitement; never in his wildest dreams did he think he would be standing beside Paul and the others on the deck of a spacecraft. The Commander then spoke in an urgent voice. They all looked at him wondering what was up!

"Please be understanding, but these Surface Earthlings must not be allowed to see the entrance into Inner Earth. These are only for those living in Inner Earth to know the secret. We are now about to enter through a gateway into Inner Earth and I ask that Paul, Misty and Arthur follow me to the quarters that don't have a view. This has to be, so that they will not know this entrance. I know there are many entrances, but each Sector has its own." Said the Commander

"Perfectly understood," came the reply from the Surface Earthlings together.

One of the Commander's men led the three friends to their quarters and stood outside on guard in case one of them just got a bit curious.

The Commander asked Carrie to come with him. He wanted to take her to where her father was being held with his henchmen. Walking towards where the men were being held Carrie started to feel that same overwhelming anxious feeling she gets whenever it had anything to do with her father, but this was a different situation ... he was locked up and she would be on the other side of the door. The Commander pressed a button that revealed a hidden two-way mirror and there was also a microphone. He told her to talk to her father and explain that they were taking him to his own Sector, where he will be dealt with. The evidence was safe and that they should not attempt to escape, as his men had orders to shoot to kill.

Carrie pressed the relevant buttons and began talking to her father explaining what was going to happen. Carrie stood and watched in amazement as her father just put his head in his hands and wept, this was most unusual for her father, but the Commander's hand on her arm made her look up.

"Don't be fooled by that act of regret, if he had any regret or one ounce of decency. he would never have blamed you. He would have owned up to it and perhaps claimed it was an accident. He is trying to get your sympathy, think about it ... what has he done to earn it? Absolutely nothing! Think what he did to you, your sister and your Aunt and Uncle ... is that a man full of regret? I have seen this so many times and it's all an act." The Commander said with a warm but firm voice.

"I know what you're saying, and I understand it. He is my father but a father I know to be so cruel and have disregard for his wife and children." Replied Carrie with anger. Turning once again towards the screen she looked at her father and just felt nothing for him.

*"Father, you will be put before our Elders who will decide your punishment for the murder and yes, I am saying **MURDER** of my beautiful, innocent mother, who did not deserve the contempt and ill treatment you delivered out to her."* Carrie said without emotion in her voice.

That seemed to get through to her father. He had no remorse, no regrets – it had been just an act he put on - because he stood up, outstretched arms placed on the table in front of him, slightly leaning forward and looking straight at her and just began shouting at her. He was livid. He was fuming. His body was shaking with the fury within him. He was threatening her that he will make sure that all of her friends and family will never testify against him. She forgets he has many acquaintances throughout the Sectors.

Carrie shook her head in disbelief her father acted as though he would never reach the courts of punishment within their Sector.

"He is right you know," said the Commander.

"What do you mean by he is right?" Carrie asked.

Commander: *"Over the many years that your father has held a high position he has made many acquaintances, many he has done favours for and they won't take kindly to him being arrested. Between us docking and getting you all back to your own Sectors, we must also expect, allow for the possibility of people trying to attempt to rescue your father. It will be an extremely dangerous journey back to your own Sector. I personally don't trust one or two of my own Elders, who by the way have no idea we are bringing back so many people, but I have contacted the Elders of your own Sector and they will be waiting for you."*

Carrie: *"If this is true how can I trust my own Elders?"*

Commander: *"Ah, did I forget to tell you that that Aunt of yours is one brave lady; she contacted several of her friends and they contacted the most trusted of the Elders, who will be there to meet you all."*

Carrie: *"Well that is different."*

They returned to the command room, where they noticed that a small fleet of crafts were approaching them. The Commander had half expected this and went over to the control panel and began engaging a narrative with the Commander of that particular fleet. Seemingly, from what Carrie could gather, they were from Sector 7 and wanted them to hand over her father and his men.

Commander Morake: *"Commander Caranda, this is Commander Morake from Sector 7* (which held the Reptilian Race) *and we have come to relieve you of your prisoners. We are in debt to Carl and we will not allow you to transport him back to Sector 1. Our Elders are requesting that you hand him over immediately to avoid any casualties."*

Commander Caranda: *"My reply to you Commander Morake is that this man is wanted for the murder of his wife. On board I have my own personnel plus 50 people from Inner Earth who are travelling back with us from the Surface Earth. Should you wish to engage, then remember this, you will need to answer to Sector 1, the highest command of all the Sectors, why you are threating their people on board."*

Commander Morake: *"We don't wish any harm to come to any of those on board, but I have my orders to take possession of your prisoner. We will not allow you to proceed."*

Commander Caranda: *"By all means try!"*

Carrie was getting worried. They were actually going into battle now, she needed to go tell the others what was happening. Maybe they had some solution to the problem facing them.

Entering the dining area she walked over to her sister, Aunt and Uncle and began explaining what was happening outside this very minute. Roberta clapped her hands for attention, upon hearing what was happening and wanted to know if they were ready to show what they were all capable of.

Carrie looked at Connie, what was her Aunt on about ... showing them what they were capable of?

Roberta watched their surprised expression, as she went over to all the women and gathered them into a circle, she beckoned for Carrie and Connie to come as well. '*What in the world was going to happen?*' thought Carrie and Connie.

"Right ladies! We all know exactly what we women are capable of.

Are you all ready to show these people what it means going against the women from Sector 1?" Asked Roberta.

"***Yes**!"* came the resounding reply from the women present, even the youngest of the females cheered on.

"Okay Carrie and Connie lead us to the Command Control section. It is about time they learned not to mess with us ever again!" Announced Roberta.

Carrie led the way to the Command Control and going towards the Commander who was standing there in shock that so many ladies where now on his deck, he asked Carrie what was going on.

But before she could even reply, Roberta explained that all the women of Sector 1 had amazing, exceptional special gifts that they never use, unless threatened in any way, they were a powerful force when all gathered together.

Commander Caranda thought about this, but still couldn't understand what they were all doing on his deck. Yes, they had explained but he didn't know what they wanted or even were going to do.

Roberta: *"Commander, those ships in front are not going to take this ship, we, the women of Sector 1 will not allow them to board and take the prisoner. He will stand trial for the murder of my sister, even if I have to drag him all the way back to the Sector on myself."*

Commander: *"What are you planning on doing, and how may I assist?"*

Roberta: *"What I want you to do is contact the Commander of the main vessel I wish to speak to him personally."*

The Commander still bewildered at what exactly was going to happen, opened the com-channel to Commander Morake.

Roberta: *"I wish to speak to Commander Morake."*

Commander Morake: *"Speaking! Who are you and what is it you enquire?"*

Roberta: *"What I want is simply for you to turn around and go back to your own Sector. Failure to comply this request, then the Women of Sector 1 will make you!"*

Commander Morake: *"How **dare** you speak to me like! **You** have no authority to demand anything! **You** cannot make me do anything!"*

Roberta: *"I dare, and I will. You have exactly five minutes to turn around and go back to where you came from or we shall make you."*

Commander Caranda was getting extremely nervous. This lady was demanding the impossible. In fact, she was actively engaging them in war. Was this trip worth the war? He drew a deep breath and walked over to Roberta, and as he did so, he noticed that the other ladies were gathering around her. Why were they doing this? What was he about to witness? What was going to happen? Mentally, he was preparing for battle. The atmosphere was electric. He stepped aside to wait and to see the outcome first.
Time seem to stand still. The ships weren't moving. Morake's fleet were still blocking the entrance and seemed to have no intention to leave.

Commander Morake: *"Commander Caranda! I command you now to hand over those prisoners or **we will open fire! Make no mistake of this!**"*

Commander Caranda was about to move forward but Roberta told him to stay still.

Roberta: *"Commander Morake. I gave you instructions to remove yourself from our path. You seem not to have gotten a clear message, then so be it!"*

Carrie and her Inner Earth people gathered together holding hands, they focused on the ships in front of them, there seemed to be like some sort of energetic beam coming from the ladies, and they were directing it to one of the ships. Still observing, he was amazed when one of the ships seemed to turn around of its own accord and go back. He watched on in amazement as now all the ships were basically turned around and forced back.

Commander Morake: *"What are you doing to my ships?"*

Roberta: *"I warned you to turn around and retreat, you didn't, so we have done that for you. Those ships are now on course back home Sector and they won't be able to turn back around. They are heading as we speak to their own docking area. I suggest you do the same. We won't be as lenient with you ... we will blow you out of the skies. We give you five minutes to turn around and head back."*

Commander Caranda watched in amazement as the lead ship turned and headed back to its own Sector. What had just happened? How did this happen? But for what it was, he was grateful to these ladies ... they had stopped a war.

Commander Caranda: *"I am not going to ask how you did that but well done ladies, a loss of life is not something I like to have happen, so I am very glad that you didn't do anything that could have led to a battle. Your people are known to be peaceful people that hold many secrets and I think I have just witnessed one of those secrets."*

Roberta, smiling: *"We never had any intention of killing anyone, as you say, we are normally a peaceful nation except for the odd one or two. But as women, we hold onto the true beliefs of our people: "Harm no one if you can help it" and we have just, I believe, demonstrated our power to those from Sector 7."*

Laughing, all the ladies left the Command Control section and made their way back to the dining room pleased with themselves. Carrie and Connie remained behind and watched as the lead ship left. Commander Caranda prepared for docking and steered towards his own Sector's landing dock.

CHAPTER 20

Sector 7

They arrived at Sector 10's landing dock and Paul, Misty and Arthur were then allowed out of their quarters, Carrie was there to greet them and told them all about the attack that never happened, but omitted about what the ladies did that was private and confidential and not for Surface Earthlings to know about.

They all disembarked, and Roberta approached the Elders from her own Sector, who were there to escort them and the prisoners to Sector 1. Roberta actually noticed one of the guards. She recognised him as being one of the guards during the time of her being held prisoner. This struck her odd – what was his business here? She walked over and led her friend, the Elder, to one side and informed him of the guard and his actions. She didn't trust him and wanted him arrested, along with Carl and his two henchmen. The Elder signalled to two of his own trusted guardsmen and informed them to take into custody the guard that Roberta had mention. The Elder and Roberta both stood and watched these men walk over to that guard and relieve him of his weapons and placed him under arrest. He argued that he had only been doing his duty when he was ordered to guard Roberta and was not loyal to Carl - it was his job and that was all. The Elder approached him and told him, if he was innocent, he had nothing to worry about. They would take him back along with Carl and his two henchmen and he could then plead his case to the High Council. Shaking, the guard nodded he knew deep inside he was in deep trouble, but he also knew that he would fight his own case and that he intended to do.

Carl and his two henchmen were escorted off the ship in restraints and handed over to the waiting guards, whose duty is now to safely return them to Sector 1 for the Hearing. Carl, looking over to his right, witnessed "his" guard being arrested and thought now his chances of escaping had just gone down a peg or two, but he still had other friends that should come to his aid.

Roberta was still taking to the Elder and introduced the Surface Earthlings, who were key witnesses to all that had happened up on the Surface of Earth and should be heard. Nodding in agreement, the Elder walked over to the Surface Earthlings and introduced himself. He welcomed them and expressed his sincere hope, that anything they would be witness to or areas they visit here in Inner Earth, could be entrusted to them to be kept quiet. Misty, Paul, and Arthur nodded in union, despite not even knowing what they would be seeing ... but they started to get excited all over again.

Roberta, resuming her conversation with the Elder, explained what they had encountered from Sector 7 and given Commander Morake's name. She went to describe what they had to do to protect themselves. The Elder stood there, looking at her in amazement; he knew the women had strange and powerful gifts, but this was unexpected and unheard of. Together, the Elder and Roberta approached two of the other Elders and gave details about the betrayal from Sector 7; they said they would personally deal with it and they waited for everyone to come forward.

Now, that all had gathered, Commander Caranda took the lead by starting to explain, that two of his men would be the one's escorting both Carrie and her sister to Sector 1, he continued stating that he would not take "no" for an answer, he felt it was his responsibility to make sure they reached the Sector and the Hearing safely.

"In that case," said Roberta very 'matter of fact', *"both myself and my husband will gladly tag along we shall all go together."*

"You are most welcome to join us," replied the Commander.

Roberta addressed the group of Elders, described how the Commander and his people had helped her escape. She highlighted that she felt, she owed her life to him and trusted him. Her niece trusts him and that is why she had no objections to follow him, along with her nieces and the Surface Earthlings. The Elders seemed to hesitate and then agreed that it was best, they should all travel together. It appeared clear that the Commander had other means to get them back safely. The Elders face each other, discussed something out of ear's shot, tuned and then started move away. Returning to their vessels, they moved out of Sector 10 and back up to their own Sector, leading the rest of the Inner Earth people and the prisoners.

Once they were out of sight the Commander explained his decision about escorting them himself with some of his crew. He didn't trust one of the Elders even though he hadn't said anything, he remembered that one of the Elders had been with Carl during a meeting and they seemed to be good friends. Roberta got worried. She wondered now if the prisoners would ever reach Sector 1, but Carrie assured her that Marco, who has a Black-Belt in Martial Arts, would make sure that they all got back safely to Sector 1!

"I have sent some of my own men to trail them until they reach the safety of Sector 1, if there is any trouble, they will contact me through this device," and held up an unusual looking device, one that would keep them in communication with the others.

"Thank you for everything you are doing for us," said Roberta.

"Yes thank you, said Carrie.

"That is quite alright, once we have this all done then my debt is paid to you for saving Katakana," said the Commander.

"Oh, does that mean we won't be able to communicate with you again?" asked Carrie

"Of course not, you misunderstand me my gratitude in saving one of my own people was beyond reproach and now my debt is just about over, but we are still friends yes and anytime you're in trouble you can always contact me." Said the Commander.

Picking up his weapons, he instructed his men to lead the way up to Sector 1. The plan was, that they would be taking a different and secret route, one that is not known to anyone other than the Commander and the two of his most trusted warriors. They began trekking. The path was in some parts steep but mostly flat. Paul, Misty, and Arthur were taking it all in, seeing the different Sectors from a distance as they followed the rest of them. At one point the Commander stopped, and communicated with his men, who were following the others. They had taken the simple route, a more direct route, and reported back that so far everything was unremarkable and that nothing had happened, but they would continue their surveillance. The Commander continue his advancing ... they should reach their own Sectors soon ... and hopefully nothing would happen, he didn't hold out much hope of an attempted rescue.

Roberta looked about her and realized they would soon be approaching their own Sector. Anxious now, she needed to have a talk with the Commander, she had to make him aware of the new defence system that had been put in place since her escape, to stop others from escaping. The Commander explained he had already known and that they would be fine. There would be friends to meet up with them once they reached the border.

Twenty minutes later they arrived at the Sector and waiting for them was no other than Katakana. Carrie was puzzled and confused and wondered how he had got here. The Commander greeted him. Katakana led them to a section where they met up with one of the Inner Earth guards, whom Katakana knew, and Carrie and her friends and Aunt and Uncle were led through the barrier. Once through, they turned around to bid the Commander and his crew farewell and followed the guard.

Walking behind the guard, Roberta was amazed that things were basically still the same, they continued walking down the path leading to the main entrance of their own Sector. Looking up Paul couldn't believe his eyes; the buildings were actually levitating above them, and he nearly tripped into Misty and Arthur who were also looking up and wondering with amazement how this could be. The guard stopped at a large door and opened it. He led them though and they boarded a shuttle. And just like that, it began to ascend, there were no rail tracks and similar, just levitating upwards. Paul clung onto the sides, wondering if they would simply plummet to the ground.

Carrie and Connie looked at each other smiling and thought: '*They hadn't seen nothing yet!*' They would see so much more but that could wait until they reached, what she hoped, was still her Aunt's home - if it hadn't been taken from her.

Roberta was thinking the same. Since her arrest she had been wondered if her beautiful home had also been taken from her and if it had, she would fight to get it back. She had done so many wonderful things to her home.

The shuttle docked at this building that they had seen above their heads and walked out onto what Paul could only describe as being glass floors, he was just amazed, they followed the others. As they passed through each section, they saw different levitating buildings, it was, they thought, like something out of a movie but this was real life.

Roberta walked straight over to the lady at the desk and when questioned, the lady announced that her home was still intact and that she would be allowed to go there and that the girl's home had also been made available for them. Roberta thanked lady but until everything was settled, they would be staying with her. Roberta didn't ask about her other dwelling, which was located elsewhere, it was a place that both herself and Armando had found and kept that one hidden. It was a safe haven for them, one that they had tried desperately to escape to before the arrest.

They all made their way towards Roberta's home, when suddenly there was a beeping sound. Carrie had completely forgotten the device that the Commander had given her. She answered it. She looked up in alarm. There had been an attempt to rescue her father! It failed; he had not escaped ... the men, the Commander had sent, had intercepted and they all, including the rescue party had been arrested ... the rescue party came from Sector 7!

Looking at her Aunt, Carrie explained as much as she could about her father's failed attempted rescue, and the Commander had also told her that there could be another attempt within their own Sector if he had friends and they needed to be cautious. At that moment Roberta made the decision to place her trust in one of her dearest of friends. They were approaching Roberta's home. She looked lovingly at it, it had not changed maybe the garden was a bit overgrown, but other than that, lovely.

CHAPTER 21

Ambush

One by one they all followed Roberta into her house. Roberta went over to the remote intercom on her desk, it was still working, but she examined for spying bugs to make sure that it was safe to use. Then she phoned her friend Kristina and explained she was back and what had occurred as briefly as she could. She informed Kristina that her nieces and three Surface Earthlings were here with her at her home, they would be staying there until the trial of Carrie's father.

Carrie wondered why she was telling this friend all of this, but she knew her Aunt would explain. Roberta ended her conversation with Kristina and turned to address all not to settle, to grab their belongings, they were all on the move again. They left the loggings and Roberta took out her shuttle and they all boarded, she had decided to move them all to her secret place, even Armando wondered what was happening.

"Right I guess you are all wondering why the change of plan," said Roberta.

"Well yes I was wondering that my dear," responded Armando.

"Simple. Kristina has told me that some of Carl's friends have been asking questions about the girl's whereabouts, they must of know they were on their way back, but Kristina didn't know how or why they were asking only telling me to be careful. Kristina will let me know by this device..." holding up a remote intercom, *"... that Carl and those men are in jail. And when the trial is about to be heard, she will inform my friend the Elder and explain we have disappeared out*

of sight until the beginning of the trial. We will make our appearance when it begins." Roberta explained.

The Surface Earthlings lost track of time being in the shuttle, there was so many wonderous things to observe, but they arrived at their destination and got out of the shuttle and followed Armando into a camouflaged building. Carrie decided to go and change, and Connie followed her. They needed to change out of the Surface Earthling clothes and into their Inner Earth traditional clothing. They left Roberta with her friend while they went to change. 20 minutes later, they both returned to join the others and Paul looked up and just stared at them. Not only had they changed clothes ... there was something different very about them. They had sort of changed. They were still Inner Earth Human form but there was like a celestial glow about them. Roberta noticed Paul's look on his face and followed his gaze and smiled. She too changed her appearance to her true identity.

The Surface Trio had not really noticed when entering Inner Earth that the people here had this glow about them; they had been too interested in getting to safety, but now they were becoming fascinated to learn more about their friends and who they really were.

Roberta now informed them that she needed to go for supplies with her husband and that they either stay in the house out of sight or they can go out into the garden area, but be vigilant, you never know if we have been followed or not. Roberta left with her husband and the others decided to go outside and talk about their different experiences, Arthur wanted to know a bit more about them and where they came from and who they were. Misty was more interested in knowing about all the different sectors and what different Aliens were there. Seemingly Paul was more interested in exploring around the house so took himself off and disappeared into the tree area out of sight.

"Firstly we are called Agarthan's and we are what you would term the future humans, I know that doesn't seem possible but that is who we are. You are our Past and we your Future. The Commander whom you met is another Alien Species, also here also to help mankind evolve. He is Epsilon Eridani. He is from the Planet Eridani B, also known as Ægir, they are here to Assist, Guide and above all help to expose any Experiential Alien that tries to take control over the Sectors. Because they are in Sector 10, they've become our last resort if things happen." Carrie explained.

"Wow, that is amazing! If there's a B-Planet, is there a A-Planet? And what you are saying, is that there are all different races within Inner Earth, some are not harmful but there are one or two that are. Did I understand you correct?" Asked Misty.

"Yes pretty much so, there are two fractions that are being closely monitored one of which we encountered on our journey back here; the ships that were trying to attack us, were Reptilian. Don't get me wrong, there are supposed to be some Reptilians that are peaceful but we have come to the conclusion, that some of the ones that are ... how shall I say ... evil, have managed get in and infiltrate and will try to take control. This is one of the reasons for Sector 10. There is another race here, they are the Essasani, they are also here to assist mankind. And yes, their main Eridani Planet is also known as Ran." Carrie replied.

Suddenly they were all interrupted by two Reptilians approaching them carrying weapons. As they advanced, Carrie and Connie became scared and wondered how on earth they had found them, then remembered her Aunties words: "... be careful we could have been followed".

Pointing their weapons at Carrie and Connie they told them that they had come for them to prevent them testifying against their father. He was an alley to them, and they had orders to take them. Carrie started to shout that she wasn't going anywhere with them. She hoped that her voice would carry to Paul who still hadn't appeared yet. Was he watching what was happening?

Paul at that particular moment had just about decided to go back and had reached the edge of the trees when he heard Carrie shouting. Ducking behind the tree he watched and saw the two Reptilians pointing guns at both Carrie and Connie and the rest of them. Creeping around out of sight, Paul made his way around until he was behind the aliens. Misty had seen him come up behind the aliens and tried to catch their attention:

"You're not taking our friends anywhere, they will attend the trial and they will see their father brought to justice, just who did you think you are bullying us?" demanded Misty.

"Earthling, I suggest that you be quiet. We haven't come for you and your friend. We are here for the two girls. If you try to resist then we have no option but to dispose of you, and that I can assure you, you don't want to have happen." Boomed back one of the Reptilians.

Misty watched as Paul approached the nearest Reptilian to him, he suddenly leapt onto the Reptilian taking him by surprise, the other Reptilian was also taken by surprise. He sees this Surface Earthling jumping on his companion, he took his eyes of the others to try to help his companion and that was the distraction needed, for Carrie raised her weapon and fired. The Reptilian collapsed, stunned, as Carrie had used the stunning part of her gun, she didn't like killing but would have done if it had to be done. Paul had also gotten the other Reptilian under control – he was out cold after applying a Jiu-Jitsu move. Connie in the meantime had run back to the house and returned with some ropes, they tied up the Reptilians and waited for their

Aunt and Uncle to come home.

What seemed like hours had passed, Roberta arrived home and was met with two tied up Reptilians and five smiling faces. The Reptilians started to wake up and tried to free themselves. Roberta went over and spoke to one of them asking what they thought they were doing, they laughed and told them that they were only the scouting party, and more were coming, and they should be arriving shortly.

Roberta stood up and looked at her husband he nodded, they walked around to the section under the house and brought out heavy laden devices; they looked like heavy-duty artillery weapons.

Carrie stared in amazement. She just couldn't believe what she was looking at. Who is Aunt Roberta and Uncle Armando? How had they even gotten their hands on these weapons and why? Going over to her Aunt and Uncle looking for an explanation, she was told that they knew one day they would need to protect themselves from invasion from other Sectors as things had been getting worse. Roberta told everyone to help them get the weapons up into the house, and ordered them to keep away from the windows, which everyone did. Going over to a part on the wall Armando pressed a secret section and it opened up, to reveal some switches and what looked like remote-control stuff. Roberta joined Armando and began pressing the necessary buttons and logging in the security codes. Suddenly the whole house was encased. They were all within a Force Shield that engulfed the house. Carrie immediately understood this was a barrier to try to keep out the Reptilians.

Once that was done Roberta decided that they all needed to eat, they would need all their strength for the battle to come. Roberta called over Carrie and Connie telling them that she had sent out distress beacon to the only people she trusted, in the hope that one of them would respond.

They all sat down to their meal, really not hungry but knew they had to eat. They chattered and decided battle plans; Paul, Arthur and Misty were told that since this wasn't their battle, they had every right to stay out of it, but they did hope that the increase in numbers would hopefully persuade the rest of the Reptilians to leave. The Trio did not even need to discuss this, they told everyone present that they had come to help their friends and would not back down now as scared as they were. All they knew is they wanted to help. Armando thanked them and gave them each a weapon, explaining how they fired and the different degrees of stun, and the kill button. As Armando was telling the Trio all about the guns and their uses, Connie had been watching out for this advancing party of Reptilians. There ... they had come out into the clearing ... she could see at least ten of them there, but there more surrounding the house ...

Carrie ran upstairs to the back and looked out. There were at least five there and she could see that more were arriving to the sides of the house, they were literally surrounded. Carrie searched in her pocket for the device that the Commander had given her and pressed the control button, the Commander answered straightaway, she told him what was happening and how many there were. She explained that her Aunt had called for help from some friends and that she had put up a barrier around the house, they had weapons and hopefully will survive. The Commander told her not to worry he was sure that her Aunt and Uncle had everything under control. He also assured her and also informed her, he was actually at this moment in the sky on a mission and was unable to come to her aid at this time. Carrie thanked him and went back down the stairs telling her Aunt and Uncle everything she had seen and how many Reptilians there where.

Roberta is puzzled; why would they send so many Reptilians to capture these girls? There was something not right about all of this, something was up. She decided to contact the Elder and tell him herself what was happening.

"Ormalek, we are under attack by Reptilians. They are wanting to take Carrie and Connie captive. I estimate at least thirty or more ... why would so many Reptilians be deployed to capture two girls? Some thing's amiss, there seems to be something not right," said Roberta.

Ormalek: *"Yes, I have just heard that Carl has friends within the Reptilian Race. It appears they have decided to capture or kidnap the girls to deny them the opportunity to testify. But what I fail to understand is why so many of them? They must be aware that they are breaking the rules by coming up to our Sector."*

Roberta: *"Has anyone checked up on Carl where he is being held? There seems to be too much action going on! Have the other races come up for the trial as well? I know the Leaders of the Reptilian and the Draconian will be there much as it grieves me, they are not what I would call a good Race. Some, when they came into Inner Earth, were peaceful, but I believe that the evil ones have infiltrated and are now controlling them.*

Ormalek: *"I do believe you are right. We have had many concerns about the increase of movement amongst the Reptilian and Draconian races, even though they are separate in different Sectors. I do believe they communicate more than we ever thought possible."*

Roberta: *"Please look into finding out if Carl is still where he is supposed to be. This could be a decoy attacking the girls."*

Ormalek: *"I shall indeed do this but first I must welcome the other races who have made their way to Sector 1 for the trial. You know the Inner Earth rules. You know that all these things have to be done fairly, and yes I know you didn't actually get a trial we are looking into that one as well."*

Roberta: *"Have you sent the investigators to find out how Carl rose to be where he is? He did that very quickly, too quickly if you ask me. Who are the influencers? What have they on him? We need to find those answers before the trial begins. It's imperative, we do. Get our best investigative hackers involved. We must not be found out!"*

Ormalek: *"We have already started the investigations and some, I must say, even surprised me. We are also investigating the bribes, the threats and such, we are currently setting up a dossier on his activities."*

Roberta: *"Oh good. One other area you should look into is his connection with the Reptilians and the Draconian. I feel there is a lot of unexplained things there."*

Ormalek - laughing: *"Your mind must be on overdrive ... "*

Roberta: *"Not on overdrive, but on survival mode."*

Ormalek: *"I will let you know as soon as we have any news and hopefully you will make it though. There are men on their way hopefully they reach you before these Reptilians get to you."*

Roberta: *"Well you have found out my secret hideaway, which to all purposes was for myself and my husband to relax, now it seems everyone will know about it."*

Ormalek: *"Very true, I saw that you had sent the co-ordinates to your secret hideaway good for you."*

Walking back into the room she looked around, everyone was at their station, they could see that the Reptilians were trying to force their way pass the Force Shield, but each time they were knocked back. They seemed frustrated and angry, but they didn't seem to be using any force to dismantle the Force Shield. Watching everything Paul was the first to notice them bring up some sort of contraption. He didn't know what it was and seemingly Armando did, as he shouted to them to get right the way back, they were using the device to try to break through the Force Shield.

Roberta knew the Force Shield could withstand a lot of things and she only hoped that this time it would stand up to this assault also. They didn't need these Reptilians to break through. One, who appeared to be the Leader, shouted that they wanted their two comrades back and that they would then leave them in peace. Armando didn't trust them. He looked around at everyone including the two captives who were enjoying the fact that their leader was demanding their release. Going over to a control switch, Roberta informed the Leader of the Reptilians, that his men would be release but only once the rest had retreated back, and that she knew how many there actually there so no tricks. Armando is intrigued. He wanted to know what she was doing, because as long as they had these two Reptilians captive, they wouldn't try to get in. Roberta told him that they would need to release the two Reptilians, but she had a plan and told him to trust her. She walked over to Paul and told him to get the two reptilians on their feet they were releasing them. Paul looked at her thinking if they shut down the Force Shield, they would just advance.

Roberta told the two Reptilians to go to the door and instructed Paul to open it. They were to step down and wait. Roberta then went over to the control room and pressed a button and to everyone's amazement a section of the Force Shield, outside where the Reptilian captives stood, allowed them to pass through which they did, and then Roberta pressed the button again and it put the Force Shield back up.

Watching from a safe distance Misty watched as the two captives were re-untied and led away, the rest of the Reptilians followed. What had just happened? They had come for Carrie and Connie and were now leaving without them. This didn't seem right. Were they up to something else? Armando was also thinking the same thing, he watched as they retreated but then saw the Leader come back. He looked menacing which seemed to frighten Connie, but he looked at the house and then walked away. Was this over? They didn't think it was.

As they watched them retreat, they saw men arriving in vehicles. It was their own men and some other aliens ... the Reptilians must have been alerted that these men were coming and had retreated not wanting to start a war.

CHAPTER 22

Grand Jury

Roberta switched of the Force Shield and went to greet the army of people who had come to their rescue. One of them was her friend, the Elder; he looked grim and worried, something had happened. Roberta knew by the look on his face.

Accompanying the Elder into her home she signalled him to take a seat and she sat down opposite him. All other house guests found their own seating arrangements and were eager to learn, what information or news Elder Ormalek was about to reveal: *"I am afraid I have extremely bad news to tell you Roberta! It appears that this Reptilian attack was a sly diversion. Remember you told me to check up on Carl? Well ... the other bad news is, he has escaped. How, we still don't know but it would seem that he had help from the said Reptilians."*

Carrie: *"You have got to be kidding! How on earth was that allowed to happen?!? He was under tight security or so I thought."*

Ormalek: *"Exactly, that's it, exactly! HOW?"*

Roberta: *"So you are telling me that Carl is on the loose and he may be hiding within the Reptilian Sector, which, as we know, will be impossible to search."*

Ormalek: *"And further to our conversation ... we have also arrested some members of the council and their associates for treason. Our investigations showed that they were the ones that had helped Carl rise to the Status he holds today. They did this for favours ... what those are we have yet to discover, but it is possible that it has* *something to do with Reptilians and the Draconian."*

Roberta: *"Right, so now we need to find out what he has on them, any possible blackmailing... maybe fraud and/or treason ... hopefully before or during the trial. Speaking of which, can the trial proceed without Carl's presence?"*

Ormalek: *"Most certainly! At the end of the day, you hold the evidence. The fact that he has escaped does not mean, he has escaped the decision of his guilt. This is why I have come to escort you all back; the trial has been brought forward and will commence in a few hours' time."*

Roberta: *"So soon? How come the rush?"*

Ormalek: *"The sooner the better! 'Cause then we can get on with finding Carl and putting him back where he belongs, and these three Surface Earthlings will be able to testify and will be taken back up once the verdict has been reached."*

Carrie: *"Have all the Races arrived?"*

Ormalek: *"Yes they have. Even two from the Reptilian and Draconian race. We know how they will be voting, so we are prepared; they will be outvoted that is for sure, we just need to protect you from here on in."*

Everyone gathered up their belongings and left Roberta's home. Ormalek led the way, outside they were greeted by their escorts and left the comfort of Roberta's home. Less than an hour later the escorted party had arrived at Roberta's home in the city, guards were placed outside, and they would stay there until they escorted them to the Hall where the trial would commence.

They remained at Roberta's for two hours before being escorted to the Hall. Here they were met by the Elders of their own people and the Grand Jury members from the other Sectors. Scanning them Roberta thought she recognized one of the Reptilian juror. This one looked very much like the one, the leader, that had come to her home ... the one in the once secret location ... , so there had been a reason for them being there... a decoy, a distraction, well it worked, she thought. What was his game? She would need to consult with Ormalek and inform him that she recognized a Juror.

As Carrie and Connie were brought to their seats, Paul, Misty, and Arthur sat directly behind them. Paul was gobsmacked. He had never seen so many aliens in his life ... well, if the truth was told, he had NEVER seen aliens in real life before. The other two were also looking around in amazement.

Roberta came into the room and sat next to Carrie and Connie. Roberta had informed Ormalek of the Reptilian leader, but he had told her not to worry, his vote would just be a vote as there were too many of the other races there to out vote him. They watched the court members enter the courtroom. After they were sworn in, the bailiff announced: "**ALL RISE!**" in a sharp voice that could be heard by all, as the Chief Elder (like the Judge on Surface Earth) entered. The Chief Elder informed all present, to listen to the proceedings and that they would be watching a holographic imagery of the evidence, one, he said, he knew many had already seen, but they would be seeing it again and that there would also be first-hand testimonies. All the jurors nodded in agreement, he then proceeded to introduce the Surface Earthlings, informing the jurors of how they had been on hand to help Carrie and Connie and that they would also give evidence.

Carrie and Connie stood up and they removed their pendants from around their neck and handed them to Roberta, who then proceeded to put them together and pressed the middle section of Carrie's half and the Hologram started to play out.

Every juror watched in silence as they listened to the voice of the mother and the father ... witnessing the physical aggression that came from this man towards this woman, his wife ... they all recognized him as being Carl, the father to these two young women ... it was clear as day that Carl had fatally injured his wife and left her to die alone. The scene was mind numbing, making many feel uneasy in their seats.

Clearing his throat, the Chief Elder then asked in turn first Paul, then Misty and finally Arthur to give evidence, and when they had done so, it was then Carrie and Connie's turn to give evidence.

Carrie started by giving a full description of everything that had happened, followed by her sister Connie. Then Roberta was to give the last piece of evidence for herself and her husband. She explained that Carl had put them in jail – hard labour camp - for no reason and how they had lost five years of their life to his cruelty.

Once all the evidence had been given Carrie, Connie, Roberta, and the Surface Earthlings left the Hall to wait outside until the deliberations was completed and the vote was taken.

It was over an hour later when they were told to come back into the Hall, the Chief Elder told them to sit down, the verdict had been reached. Slight unrest was noticed, and the bailiff called for **QUIET**, as the Head Juror of the Grand Jury was now going to read the verdict:

"In the first instance the death of your mother, we find Carl guilty as charged. In the second instance of the unlawful incarceration of Roberta and Armando, we also find him guilty as charged." We the "The Council of Elders" have cautioned each Sector that should they harbour Carl then they will face the highest penalty and be exiled from Inner Earth." Chief Elder proclaimed.

Looking around the room Carrie was thankful of the decision; Roberta was not looking around but looking directly at the Reptilian and the Draconian jurors. They were talking with each other which was strange, the Reptilian Leader looked over to Roberta and there was hatred there for all to see. Armando also had observed the Reptilian Leader looking towards his wife, he knew that although Carl had been found guilty it was not over yet - it had just really begun, with Carl on the loose the girls would never be safe.

Leaving the Hall together everyone made their way to Roberta's home. When Roberta entered her home and she sank down into the chair, feeling despair, desperate, frustrated, and exhausted. She knew herself deep within that the war had only just begun, what would come next ... the look from that Reptilian Leader said it all, it was definitely not over.

Paul walked over to Roberta and began asking about Marco and if there was a possibility that he could actually see him, he hadn't seen him since they entered Inner Earth and was anxious to see his friend and boss. Roberta told Paul that she would contact Marco's mother but for now they all need rest and food. Paul agreed he was hungry and tired it had been a lot to take in and was wondering if they would be here much longer or would they leave as soon as possible, it seemed with Carl at large they may would have to wait.

Carrie and Connie were sitting talking about their father, they knew with him being unrestrained they wouldn't be safe. Despite the whole of Sector 1 knowing about their father there was no way of knowing how safe they would be ... always be wondering when he was going to surface ... could they even go back to their own home?

Roberta honed in on their thoughts and walking over to them she suggested that they all have a walk over to their family home and see how they felt about it. They had friends who would most certainly protect them and there would be guards place there to protect them, maybe they need their own space, and she would like to think their Surface friends would also like to see where the girls lived.

After talking with her Aunt and Uncle, Carrie took her sister and their friends to her own home, she wanted to see how much it had changed, knowing her father she knew things would have changed, all her mother's things would have gone or would they.

Paul followed everyone out as they walked over to Carrie's home followed by two guards who as Roberta had told him would be accompanying Carrie and Connie until their father was caught.

On entering her home Carrie was surprised that nothing had really changed, the only thing that had changed was that there was another lady in the home. Who was this she? Surely not her father's new wife? The woman looked hostile towards the girls, demanding what on earth they were doing in her home, what right had they, to enter it? Hadn't they done enough damage, having their father taking the blame and go on the run? Carrie was not the girl she had been when she had first left her home, she looked at the woman with distaste.

"How dare you accuse my sister and myself of entering ***your*** *home! This is not your home this Is* ***our*** *home, and that of our deceased mother!* ***You*** *have no right to be here and I ask you kindly to leave!"* exclaimed Carrie.

"You're asking me to kindly leave? Hah, how dare you! Just how dare you! This is my home now. I coupled with your father two years ago and made this my home, so now I ask YOU to leave!" demanded the lady.

Turning to the guards who had just entered hearing the exchange of words and ordered them to remove the lady now.

"I must contact Ormalek to ask his guidance on this matter," said one of the guards.

"Please, do as you please, if you think you must." said the lady.

Connie was getting really annoyed now and left the house and walked back to her Aunties explaining what was going on, Roberta fuming marched back over with Connie and was entering the home, when she could hear the arguments that was erupting within.

"I order you to leave this home now, this is no longer you home!" The woman said with raised voice.

Roberta recognized the lady at once she had always had that feeling that Carl was secretly having what the Surface Earthlings would class as an affair and now here in front of her was the evidence. Walking over to this woman, Roberta told her this house in fact didn't even belong to Carl but belonged to her late Sister. It had been handed down to her from their parents, as had her home. Carl had no rights to this house and neither had she and she must go and pack her belongings and remove herself before she was removed by force. Red faced and so angry the woman marched out and into the bedroom with Carrie following her; Carrie wanted to make sure that she only took what belonged to her and nothing belonging to her mother.

This lady whose name is Selina, was gathering up her belongings and she went over to what Carrie knew to be her mother's jewellery box and began to pack it away. Carrie marched over and grabbed it off her and opened it up to reveal her mother's jewellery. No way was she taking them!

"You only take what belongs to you personally and nothing that belongs to my mother or you will find yourself up before the High Council do I make myself clear?" Carrie said with a hard tone in her voice. Selina turned to look Carrie straight in the eyes and replied: *"Crystal clear you ungrateful bitch! You are some daughter! What kind of a daughter would have her father arrested for something he hadn't done?"*

Carrie did not respond, she was still fuming when she marched Selina back into the main room, telling her Aunty what she had tried to do and the comment about her father. Roberta stood there, looking at Selina ... contemplating her next step ... drew a deep breath and walked over to a place on the shelf, that even Carrie and Connie didn't know about, pressed a switch and suddenly the same Hologram played over again for all to see. Selina stood and watched in total disbelief. Mortified. What had Carl done? Why? What else had Carl lied about? She felt betrayed, humiliated, and angry. She hadn't realized the full actions of her new husband. How could he have done such a thing? After a few moments of total silence, Selina turned to face the girl: *"Please forgive me Carrie, please forgive me Connie. I had no idea ... I really didn't know the extent of what he had done ... of course I will leave! I will go now to my mothers and explain everything to her."* Selina said with remorse in her voice. Walking out of the door, Selina smiled. She had put on such an act that they actually believed her. How wonderful! Now she had to find Carl and tell him what had just gone down, and more importantly about that hidden panel ... a stroke of genius.

Roberta watched as Selina walked away, she had always had a 6th sense when people were lying, and that woman was lying through and through. Hopefully, she will try to make contact with Carl, but she wouldn't do that straightaway, Roberta was so sure of that.

CHAPTER 23

Blue Marco

Carrie was also anxious. Who was Selina trying to kid? She had walked away so full of regret that it she knew had to be false. What was she planning? Carrie was also worried as she had been keenly watching her Aunt go to that panel and switch on the hologram; that was vital evidence.

Roberta was thinking much the same thing. The whole device must be removed but where to? It had to be somewhere in the house that even Carl or even Selina would not think of, she would have to get her husband Armando to dismantle it and put it somewhere else, but where?

Carrie suddenly came up with a suggestion; why not place it in the girls' bedroom, behind where their clothes are kept, there was enough room for Armando to remove a panel and replace it there. Roberta thought that to be a good idea and left to go fetch her husband. They must do it right away before anything else occurred, because she had the feeling that Selina and Carl would surface again together and try to get to the device.

Paul asked Roberta if she had managed to locate Marco and when could they meet up.

"Marco will call here tomorrow he knows where Carrie's home is after talking to his mother," replied Roberta.

"Oh good, it will be lovely to see my friend and discuss what is going to happen as he has a business up on the Surface of Earth and wasn't sure at the time what he was going to do with it." Said Paul.

"I am sure he will put your mind at rest. Don't forget, he hasn't lived in Inner Earth even though conceived here, he was born and lived till now, on Surface Earth," said Roberta.

"Very true, may I ask you another question, Roberta? Will his features have changed like Carrie and Connie's have or will he still be the same Marco that I know?" asked Paul.

"Well that you shall have to discover when you meet him, don't forget those born in Inner Earth or are of Inner Earth lineage will have some characteristics of Inner Earth, if he stays long enough I would say, yes, his appearance will change to that of our people," answered Roberta.

Paul was left there considering all that had just taken place. Misty and Arthur were laughing thinking it was all funny, he stood there for a moment ... staring at them before he started to laugh also. After a while Arthur asked: *"Carrie when do you think we will have to go up on the Surface Earth?"* Carrie: *"That depends on our Higher Elders. They will be working things out now, they will be considering the fact that you have seen Inner Earth, but don't worry when you go up to the surface you will have the company of myself and Connie."*

"You're going back up to the Surface?" Misty asked somewhat surprised.

"Of course we are! Don't you realize with our father on the loose and myself and Connie aren't safe here, we would be much safer on the Surface." Replied Carrie.

"Oh, never thought of that one, so what are your plans for your life on Surface Earth? Certainly you won't be able to go back to your old jobs and our flat; maybe you will need to move again, somewhere where your father can't follow you to ... well, I say follow you ... he did pretty good job in tracing you this time around." Misty said as matter of fact.

"Where are you planning on going then?" pipped up Arthur

coming into the conversation.

Carrie: *"Well certainly not in the main cities of America ... too many surveillance cameras. Maybe we should try moving to the countryside, like you know maybe a farm. I've been studying agriculture and farm life when I had nothing to do while waiting for my exams and I think Connie and myself would be safe on like a homestead."*

Arthur: *"Wow can I come?"*

Paul: *"Why in the world would you want to live on a farm?"*

Arthur: *"Why ever not? Farms have animals and horses I love horses and would also be able to keep an eye on the girls."*

Giggling Misty applauded Arthur's endeavours to keeping the girls save, was he by any chance in love with one of them? She wouldn't put that past him but hoped he wouldn't be disappointed because she had the strangest feeling, that they only married their own kind but again, she could be wrong. Arthur was the same age as Connie but advanced for his age hence he was always doing the odd wheeling and dealing. Carrie had also noticed Arthur was besotted with Connie. Are these feelings being returned, Carrie was thinking ... she need to find out from her sister as she had caught her looking in Arthur's direction on more than one occasion. Carrie would also have to have a talk with her Aunty, 'cause if for any reason a union was made between Arthur and her sister would that be allowed being that he was from the Surface of Earth and she from the Inner Earth? And just out of curiosity it would also work for her if she ever found the right man.
Carrie showed Paul and Misty to a guest room. Arthur would occupy their room and Connie and herself would sleep what she classed as her mother's room. After a small bite to eat they all retired to their rooms, everyone was on alert: they all hoped nothing would happen to destroy this bit of peace and quiet.

After a sleepless night Carrie woke and went to prepare the

breakfast only to find that Misty was there waiting to help her, so the girls arrange a breakfast before calling everyone to eat. Everything seemed too quiet, but they put that down to being too nervous of everything that had happened over the past few weeks and especially the last day or two. As they sat one of the guards came in to tell them that someone called Marcos was asking for entry into the home. Carrie went out and greeted Marco assuring the guard that it was fine he was a friend of hers.

Marco entered and looked around and seeing Paul at the breakfast table rushed over to greet his friend; to Paul's relief it was still the same Marco.

Marco: *"How are you all? I hear you's had a bit of excitement and I missed it all!"* laughing out loud.

Paul: *"Well yeah ... but how are you and your family settling into life in Inner Earth?"*

Marco: *"Hahaha, well let me put it this way I never knew I had such a large family down here, it's been a none stop of visits."*

Paul: *"What are your plans now?"*

Marco: *"To be honest Paul, one half of me is wanting to stay here but the other half is wanting my life back up on the Surface. I know my father and mother want me to stay, my sister is like me ... she has spent that much time on the Surface of Earth, and she is finding it hard to adjust but is happy to give it a go for a few months."*

Paul: *"Thank goodness so are you going to go back up to the Surface Earth."*

Marco: *"Yes I am, but I will still come and visit my parents down here. I can't get away from my birth rights."*

Paul: *"Did you hear that Carl, Carrie's father, has escaped?"*

Marco: *"We all heard about that. Hard not to. Many are a bit scared with what he might be or is going to do. He could cause so much damage. I also hear he is friends with the Reptilians and the*

Draconians, which to be honest I'd never heard of. We all here about these aliens on Surface of Earth, but to actually know they exist here in Inner Earth, makes my skin crawl." Marco is shuddering with the thought.

Paul: *"You know something, I was wondering if your appearance would change to that of Carrie and Connie's but I'm glad it hasn't."*

Marco: *"Oh, you don't think so?"*

Paul watched in amazement as his features changed just like Carrie and Connie. Laughing, Marco changed his features back

Paul: *"How on earth did you do that?"*

Marco: *"My father showed me and my sister how tor. They told us, when they were on the Surface Earth and they had to fit in, they changed their features to Surface Earthling features."*

Carrie and Connie watched the changed how features and went over to Marco and asked him to explain how he was able to suddenly change his features to that of Inner Earth people, when he hadn't known he was one. Marco explained that when they were young their parents had wanted us to have a "normal" life on the Surface, and so as we grew older, our parents noticed that we had the same features of the Surface Earthlings, when they realized this they were pleased. And now, because we came into Inner Earth and we are of Inner Earth, our features changed to match that of our species if that makes sense. Carrie knew that it made perfect sense and explained in more detail how it all worked. She also told Marco that because of her father escaping, she and her sister would also need to go back up to the Surface, but not to their old jobs or even where they had lived. They are thinking of moving either to another State or just out into the Countryside, somewhere rural, away from Washington, preferably out to a farm and become farmers with horses and cattle, chickens, and the sort. Marco said he thought that to be a good idea and they all sat around the table planning their trip back to the Surface. Marco came up with a few suggestions that looked promising, but until they were back up on the Surface of Earth, they couldn't actually find that perfect piece of land.

CHAPTER 24

Gifts

While the friends were weaving plans, elsewhere, Carl was situated in quarters provided by the Reptilians. He was fuming. His daughters had outwitted him, but thankful that the acquaintances he had made within the Reptilian world had come to his rescue. What they wanted from him in return, he would soon find out as Reptilians, he discovered a long time ago, never did anything unless it was of benefit to them. No doubt he would learn of their demands soon enough. Carl sat waiting. He was sure that it wouldn't be too long before the Reptilian Leader made an appearance and told him what was in store for him, but one thing he knew for certain: he was not going to let anyone get the better of him ever again.

Carl also had plans himself. Patiently he waited for the Reptilian Leader to join him. Carl was eager to learn what he was wanting and in turn Carl would also tell him of his own plans ... he was going to take over the whole of Inner Earth and for that he knew he needed the assistance of the Reptilians and the Draconians. So he sat and he waited. He had all the time in the world. While locked up, he had been festering , his mind had been going around in circles. He knew he had one person he could trust, a person no-one would suspect and that was Selina. He knew he could rely on her to make contact with him, when she felt it was safe to do so. As for his two girls ... he swore he would get even with them, even if it was the last thing he did.

Back, at the family home, Carrie also was thinking about her father. She knew he wouldn't stop until he got even with them both. Carrie didn't want her Surface friends involved, that is why she wanted to move away into the countryside to a farm; it may come boring, but it was better than the wrath of her father.

Paul was asking about all the Aliens that resided in Inner Earth and even Marco became interested, so Carrie started to explain each of the races and their roles.

- *"As you know we are the Agarthans and future humans, then we have*
- *the Reptilians: those you have already come across; they are used to conquering and doing mass destruction of everything they come across.*
- *The Andromedan race are here to guide and protect but they are also very spiritual; then we have*
- *the Venusians. When on earth you will have heard mention of Commander Ashtar. Well think of him when you think of the Venusians.*
- *Epsilon Eridanii: this is the Commander's race – their role is to assist and guide, but they are also here to help to expose the likes of the Reptilians and the Draconians - exposing their plans for Inner Earth or the Surface of Earth or both.*
- *The Pegasians are also protectors and help guide others.*
- *Altairians, also a race of humans who have the tendency to observe and use many technologies that the Surface humans would never even think of.*
- *The Draconians are the masters in genetic engineering and would not hesitate to abduct and experiment on the Surface Humans.*
- *The Cygnusian are also here to assist but they are highly evolved in science and do a lot exploration in this type of field.*
- *And lastly the Essasani, now these are spiritual and assist and guide whoever comes to them."* Carrie explained.

"Wow ... wow ... gosh that is a lot to take in ... wow!" Marco and Paul said at the same time.

"Yes, many different species but there are many more out there in the Universe, but these are the ones currently in Inner Earth." Carrie had a slight grin on her face.

Roberta had walked in while Carrie was giving them a history lesson so to speak of Inner Earth, she walked over to Carrie and whispered in her ear, that Paul, Misty, and Arthur must now go before the High Council. They will be fine ... only that the Council needed to talk to them, she said. Smiling, Roberta looked across at Carrie's friends and went over to Marco and said she was glad to see him once again.

Connie: *"We have been making plans."*

Roberta: *"Have you really and what may I ask what those plans are?"*

Connie: *"Well, since our father is on the run and we know we are not safe here even with the guards, we have decided that the most sensible thing to do is to go back up to the Surface and relocate ourselves."*

Roberta: *"May I ask where or what you are thinking of going or doing?"*

Connie: *"Sure. Carrie has suggested that we move out of Washington and go somewhere far away to another State, to be more exact go live on a farm with animals and horses oh, and Arthur will be coming with us."*

It seems her nieces had grown up. She was also pleased that they were returning to Surface Earth; she would feel much happier, if they were away from Inner Earth for their own safety ...

Roberta: *"Paul, Misty, and Arthur would you be so kind as to follow me to see the High Council, as the Elder wishes to have a chat with you, nothing to be afraid of. Carrie, Connie and myself will also* *be there, Marco you can also come along if you so wish since you are here."*

They all left together, following Roberta to the shuttle to see the High Council Elder who was expecting them. Upon reaching their destination Roberta led the way to a door and on opening it there were like chambers - it looked something out of this world.
Walking towards the High Elder, Roberta bowed her head and she encouraged the rest to follow her lead, Paul and the others were getting a bit nervous, what on earth where they doing here? Roberta came over smiling reassuring them all was fine, that because they had helped two of their own people, the Elders had decided to endower them each with a certain power; each would be different to the other but together they would be a force to be reckoned with.

'How was this possible, how would this work?' thought Misty as she took her position in the glass chamber, and as she stood there she felt a sort of tingling sensation and then the door was opened and Paul entered the same thing happened to him then it was Arthurs turn. Roberta was speaking to the Elder who nodded his head towards Arthur, he now felt a powerful tingling sensation and then the chamber door opened, and he exited.

"Each of you have been given a certain power: Paul you have the gift of second sight. Misty: the gift of hearing from a great distance, and lastly Arthur: he has both them gifts but also another gift - the gift of strength. You may ask why Arthur has been given more, that is because he will become Carrie and Connie's protector from now on. Both Paul and Misty, you can now assume your normal lives well sort of, but always remember your gifts must be used only when there is danger." This was the proclamation of the High Elder and then he left the room.

"Wow, that was so intense," said Paul, *"and I am glad that Arthur has those special gifts as he may just need them, if ever Carl*

finds the girls once again."

They all went back to Carrie and Connie's home, Marco said he would go and say goodbye to his mother, father and sister and join them to go back up to the Surface of Earth. Carrie and Connie went to pack, they would need almost all of their clothes and some other gadgets, like the self-protection ones, only to be used to defend themselves. These gadgets must never be shown to the Surface Humans as they were far too advance even for them.

Paul, Misty, and Arthur gathered up their few possessions and sat down and waited for Marco. There was something amiss. They remember how they got to Inner Earth, well, not really, they were in windowless rooms at the time, but how were they going to get back up to the Surface of Earth?

Roberta came back into the room just as Marco returned, he had said his farewells to his parents and sister, promising to come back to see them. Roberta led them out and down some roads to an entrance that only was visible when Roberta put a device against the wall, she was about to but seemed to hesitate, she was looking around, she could feel a presence. Stepping back Roberta passed the group and started to backtrack she saw a shadow and went over to it and there was Selina crouching down trying to make herself small. *Why are you following us?"* Roberta wanted to know.

"I'm not following you. I just happen to be on this path and saw you all so held back, what 's the problem?" Selina answered with a question.

"The problem I have is you following the girls. Go back I suppose to Carl, and don't even try to deny it I know you are lying as does Carrie," said Roberta.

"I'm not lying! Why would you think I want anything to do with that man after he deserted me?" Selina tried extremely hard to convince Roberta.

Roberta took out a device from her pocket and aimed it at Selina who was now terrified, but Roberta knew exactly what she was doing. The device was a sleeping device; when Selina woke up, she wouldn't know why she was there in the first place. Once finished with Selina, Roberta went back to the wall placed a different device and the wall seemed to part and she told them all to go through and follow the path. When they reached the steps, to continue upwards, and at the top would be a doorway, she handed Carrie another device and explained when they reached that doorway to put the device on where the handle was, and it would open for them.

She began to explain this was a dimensional doorway once they passed through it, then it would disappear they wouldn't be able to come back that way the only way back would be the way Carrie used to come, this was more direct and would put them a ten minute walk to Maroc's Martial Arts Studio.

Hugging her two nieces she told them go through the opening and back to the Surface of Earth. Roberta walked away glad that at least they would be gone, but she knew the fight hadn't even begun. She knew what Carl had planned and she shuddered to think about it, but one thing she did know her nieces would be for the time being safe. She had given Carrie a small device that if ever she need her, she would be able to contact her and vice versa.

CHAPTER 25

Re-unification

Carrie, her sister, and friends has, as predicted by her Aunt, emerged a stones-throw away from Marco's Martial Arts Studio and Paul and Misty's apartment. They made tracks towards there knowing, that even though they had made it this far, they didn't really know what was next on the agenda or what was in store for Carrie and Connie. On reaching Marco's Studio they looked around, nothing had really changed. Marco took out his keys and opened the door to his Studio. It was his pride and joy, and he knew he had made the right decision for the time being anyway. Paul also entered looked around everything was as it should be. Misty was standing at the door waiting for him so they could go up to their apartment and settle in.

They entered the apartment, and the first thing Arthur did was go to the laptop situated on the desk and began loading it up, he wanted to get started right away looking for the right place. They needed to get away before they were discovered here. Arthur looked at Texas for a place. There were many farms, but he had to find one that was for rent/sale, he was intent on finding the right one, they needed to be away from people but not too far away from a town for supplies like a small hamlet maybe. Paul was smiling at Arthur he was really getting to grips with his new task of finding the suitable place for Carrie, Connie, and himself. He hoped it would be that far away for visits but then again, he felt that visits might not happen for a while. Arthur suddenly sprung to his feet. What had he found that had made him so excited? Arthur beckoned them all over to have a look at what he had found: a nice farm with animals and yes, his most precious thing, horses. Well one horse would be available, but Arthur was sure that they could build up a fair size farm. They all came to have a look and as they viewed the online details, they were sure, that this wasn't a farm but a ranch. Carrie looked excited. Could they afford it? Even Connie was getting excited. She had never had the chance of riding a horse and now hopefully she may even get that opportunity. She had seen them in magazines but never seen one up close in person.

There was a knock at the door, and they all froze. Paul went to answer it. There standing was no other than Geraldine, she entered the room looking around at everyone.

Geraldine: *"Where have you all been? I've been searching for you all. I have had to stay with the old lady in our former place."*

Arthur: *"Well, Geraldine, it's like this. We have just come back from Inner Earth ..."*

Geraldine: *"So I have obviously missed it all then.... What do you mean by "Inner Earth"?"*

Misty: *"What are you doing here anyways? Thought you and lover boy were happy as anything?"*

Geraldine suddenly started to cry. Misty ran over to her putting her arms around her wondering what on earth could have made her cry like that.

Geraldine: *"He dumped me! H found someone else and told me to get out of the apartment, even though I've been paying most of the rent for the last few month, I had nowhere to go so came here."*

Paul: *"You've done the right thing."*

Geraldine then smiled and wanted the full details of everything she had missed. So sitting her down in a corner Misty explained everything that had happened, and how lucky she wasn't there when those Reptilians came, she would have freaked out. Bringing Geraldine up to speed, Misty also explained that right now, Arthur was looking at what he thought was a farm, when in actual fact it is a ranch, and maybe one, that Carrie, Connie and himself where going to try to lease or buy, whichever the vendors wanted and it all depended on the pricing. Geraldine got up and walked over to the laptop and looked at this farm/ranch. She liked the look of it and where it was situated. What she had never told anyone was that she grew up on something similar and loved horses. Geraldine just turned to face Carrie and asked if it was possible that she also could come. She was sick of the city life and wanted some place to relax and get back to herself, find herself. The town looked good and wasn't that small - it would do for all their needs and the next place along was about an hour's drive away, that would be the next biggest place where they could possibly get jobs if they wanted to, but first off they needed to contact the vendor to find out what he/she wanted for the ranch.

Arthur sent an email asking for more details about the purchase or the leasing of the said ranch. They just sat back. The vendor would possibly take time to get back to them, but the one thing that was bothering them, was funds.

Carrie, Connie, and Geraldine had savings, but what about Arthur? Did he have any money to speak about? they knew little of what Arthur did and whether he had savings, but they would find out in the next few days, that they were sure of.

They were still sitting around when there was another knock on the door and this time it was Marco, he came in smiling, telling them all that his students had really missed them and couldn't wait to get back to training. He walked over to Paul and asked if he was ready to start work again, the first students will be coming early tomorrow morning. Paul told him he would be ready and began to explain what Carrie, Connie, Arthur and even Geraldine had found. Marco just then noticed Geraldine for the first time standing beside Arthur.

"Why so far away?" asked Marco.

"Well we want to get as much distance from Washington as we can. We realise that my father may know this area a bit better now and be able to track us if he ever comes up to the surface or sends his spies. And so to keep our friends here safe, we decided to move to Texas." Replied Carrie.

"Sure, that is logical," said Marco.

"Look at this ranch, Marco. Tell me honestly what you think of it. We have contacted the vendor and now awaiting his decision - either leasing or buying, which ever works out the cheapest for us all." Said Arthur

Marco went over to the laptop and looking at the ranch and all the details. He was impressed that Arthur had managed to find somewhere near to a town and not too far away from a city. So now it was just a matter of waiting for the reply from the said vendor, then they could make plans to get there, they knew the journey would be a long one. Carrie needed to check something also she wanted to see if there was a place nearby that was a location to re-enter Inner Earth.

She took out the device that her Aunty Roberta had given her, punched in where this ranch was going to be and was greatly surprised that the nearest entrance was only one hour away, this made her feel better. If anything should go wrong, she could easily get herself and sister back into Inner Earth and back to the safety of her Aunt Roberta. Contacting her Aunt Roberta she explained their position and told her once they got settled, she would give her the coordination to the location of the Ranch.

"No don't do that there is a bit of trouble brewing down here so everything will get monitored, don't contact me unless it's an emergency I can't say too much but be careful is all I want to say." Was Roberta's reply.

"You've got me worried now," replied Carrie.

"Don't worry ... I know where you ... and your friends are. If ... I need to contact you ... then they can ... do that for me ... all I say is be careful..." Replied Roberta and the conversation ended abruptly.

Going over to where the others were, she explained her brief conversation with her Aunt, and they all agreed it was time to move on; time seemed to be of the essence. Marco told them he would make arrangements to get the necessary transport for them it would have to be by road as airports, and trains stations had CCTV and they would be picked up straightaway.

They all looked at Marco. There was only four of them travelling once they got the go ahead from the vendor so it would only be necessary to get a car. This was probably the best and quickest mode of transport and less costing on petrol/diesel whichever was gotten. As they all sat and waited for the vendor to contact them, they decided the best thing to do was have something to eat and relax, there was nothing they could do until they got the vendor to state his terms. Four hours later they received the long-awaited email from the vendor. He had stated that they could rent the ranch for six months which at the end of the six months if they were still keen to buy then he would take of the amount they had been renting for off the sale price he now left it in their court the price for the lease was $1,700 per month. Carrie thought that was fair enough and they responded that thank you they would like to take him up on his offer and would forward the necessary funds which they reckoned would be $2,400 by bank transfer in the morning but they would like for him to forward the legal documents before the transfer so they could sign it and for him to put his own signature on as well. The vendor said that would be fine. He would send over the legal documents first thing in the morning once he had been to see his solicitor and that they would receive the necessary papers to sign and he would also have all the bank details with the legal document, so that all they needed to do was forward it to that bank. He looked forward to seeing them to hand over the keys.

Arthur was thrilled and he was jumping up and down everyone could see he was thrilled especially when he went over to Connie and lifted her in the air and swung her around. Connie was a bit taken aback but was also now laughing, she felt a tingling sensation when Arthur was holding her.

So now a new chapter in the lives of Carrie, Connie, Arthur and not forgetting Geraldine, begins. Follow us in the next instalment to find out what happens.

APPENDIX

FIRST CHAPTER OF BOOK 2

CHAPTER 1

The New Home

Carrie, Connie, and Geraldine woke up the following day, Arthur was already up and printing off the document for the renting of the ranch. He noticed all their names were on the document and the covering letter indicated that each of them had to sign it to make it legal.

Once the document was signed by each of them, they scanned it and attached to the return email to the vendor. The vendor's name is Mr Colin Jameson; once that was done, they all got dressed and ready to go to the bank. They needed to transfer the money and get the receipt for the transaction so that they could then email the receipt to the vendor.

After having been to the bank, they all returned to Paul and Misty's apartment pleased with themselves and Arthur emailed the receipt over to the vendor. Within half an hour they got an email back saying that he was satisfied and that once they reached the town closest to the ranch to phone him. He gave his phone number and informed them he would meet them and take them to the ranch.

Carrie told them all to go and pack, she asked Paul to go and see if Marco had managed to get them sorted out with a vehicle. Paul left the apartment returning five minutes later with the keys to a reliable car that was initially owned by Marco's father who wouldn't needed it anytime soon. Marco asked if Arthur would let him have his motorbike in exchange for the car. Arthur was only too happy to hand the keys over to his motorbike; he was looking forward to driving the car - he was possibly the only one that could drive it - anyways so in all matter of fact it would become his.

Once everyone was packed up, they headed downstairs, the car was sitting on the road, Marco was standing there swinging the keys in his hand, he handed them over to Arthur and Arthur in turn handed over the keys to the motorbike. They all got in but not before the tearful farewell from Misty who told them to keep in touch and any trouble let them know. So the four friends set off on the long haul to Texas wondering what lay ahead of them. This was an adventure for Arthur and Geraldine, but for Carrie and Connie it was to put as much distance between their father and them, for he would come after them that was for sure, but when and how remained to be seen.

It took them twenty-four hours to reach their destination especially after the pit stops for some refreshments and amenities, they were glad to arrive. Arthur had contacted the vendor of the ranch when they were two hours away from their destination, he directed them to the small town and told them he would meet them in Sally's Café on the main street.

They parked the car and went over to Sally's Café to meet the vendor. Mr Jameson was sitting at a table with papers and such, he looked up as they all came in. At first, he seemed startled at these young people and at didn't give them much attention ... thought them to be just a bunch of people stopping on their travels.

At the counter they asked for Mr Colin Jameson. The man looked up and hailed them over.

Mr Jameson: *"I'm Mr Jameson. What can I do for you folks," he commented*

Arthur: *"Hello, Mr Jameson you told us to meet you here to pick up the keys to the ranch."*

Mr Jameson: *"You're the people wanting to rent the property, what do you know about farming and taking care of the Horses?"*

Arthur: *"We may be young, but Geraldine was brought up on a farm and knows the way around it. The rest of us are keen to learn everything there is to know about managing a ranch, I know we look like city slickers, but we are hard workers, and will make it work."*

Mr Jameson: *"It's your funeral as long as you can meet the payment, but you may have to also take on other paid jobs to help run the ranch."*

Arthur: *"Don't worry about that, these girls will be the ones working to bring in the extra money while I run the ranch, although they will be helping as well."* Arthur was grinning from ear to ear.

Mr Jameson: *"If you follow me then youngsters then I will show you the way and show you around the place, so you know what's what."*

Getting up he led them outside and told them to follow

him, he leapt into a jeep and waited for them to get into their car then moved out up the road, they followed him until he turned off onto, what actually looked like a dirt track. The car was having a hard time keeping up with the jeep, but Arthur was determined that he would keep up no matter what. They finally, after thirty minutes, reached the edge of the ranch itself. Outside the entrance, the jeep had stopped, and Mr Jameson was standing waiting for them. Arthur and the others got out of the car and wandered over to Mr Jameson, he spread his hands indicating the boarder of the ranch itself. You could see the ranch at the end of the road.

Mr Jameson then got into his jeep and the others got into their car, they drove to the porch of the ranch and as they got out, they were thrilled. The ranch looked as lovely as it had done on the photographs.

Mr Jameson handed the keys over to Arthur and invited him to open the front door and they all went inside, it was beautiful inside, very homely, it was furniture which actually surprised them, but they were thrilled to know that they wouldn't have to buy furniture. Mr Jameson gave them a guided tour of the kitchen, the living room they had already seen, the study which he explained was basically for the running of the ranch where all the business was done. Going upstairs he showed them four bedrooms and they were big especially for the size of the ranch. They all came back down-stairs and Mr Jameson took out some paperwork and told them to keep it safe. These were the papers for the lease, he liked them to have originals not this email jargon stuff.

He then left them promising if they needed his advice for anything, he would gladly help them.

Arthur and the girls then went out to the car and fetched all their belongings, and they went to choose their respectful bedrooms.

After they had unpacked, they decided that maybe they should have a good look around and discover what was on the ranch. He was sure he had heard some chickens when he had first got out of the car, if that was the case then they could make an omelette to have with some of the supplies they had already gotten in the last town before meeting up with Mr Jameson. They found the chickens and Arthur being the bravest went into the coop and came out with a big grin and some fresh eggs. They had a look in the barn and found a horse inside. Further looking around they spied in the field two cows so fresh milk was on the agenda marvellous, only thing being nobody knew how to milk a cow...

This ranch lark wasn't going to be easy, but they would make it. They were all young and healthy and the fresh air would do them a world of good, plus knowing for the moment they were safe.

Carrie and Connie felt a sense of relief that at last for the time being anyways they didn't have to think about their father, he hopefully wouldn't find them for an exceptionally long time, if ever.

Later that day they enjoyed a good meal and tired, they all went to their separate bedrooms and slept. Early the following morning Arthur was up sharp, collecting what eggs that were there, Connie was helping lay the table, just as Carrie and Geraldine came downstairs to fresh coffee, soft boiled eggs, and toast. The day was starting off to be grand, they felt rested and wanted to get on with learning about ranch life, Geraldine said she would go and find out how tame the horse was, as it would be good to feel a horse under again and it was a good way also to travel around the farm to see what else there was.

Made in the USA
Middletown, DE
11 April 2021

36519940R00109